Free Rein Series

New Beginnings

Christine Meunier

Free Rein Series
New Beginnings

by Christine Meunier

National Library of Australia Cataloguing-in-Publication Data

Meunier, Christine

New Beginnings

1st ed. 2013

ISBN – 978-0-9875332-2-7 (pbk.)

Cover design by Metuschaël and Christine Meunier
Cover photo by Cait O'Pray with thanks to Lori Crandell-Miller

Foreword

Whilst working to promote my first novel that was released in July 2013, I had been pondering the idea of writing a horse series for pre-teens. I wanted to be able to combine my love of horses and my faith in a series that would encourage and teach younger readers.

It amazed me how quickly *New Beginnings* formed after I was given the idea of using two characters – Geordie and Hannah – from the novel *Horse Country*.

I'm pleased to think that I can now develop these characters further whilst at the same time introducing readers to the joys of owning a first pony and learning alongside them.

I pray this series will be a source of entertainment, encouragement and enlightenment for many readers in the years to come.

Christine

Free Rein Series

1. New Beginnings
2. In Pursuit of a Horse
3. Free Reign
4. Learning to Fall
5. A Dollar Goes a Long Way
6. Contagious
7. Broken

Also by Christine Meunier

Horse Country – A World of Horses

B and B

The Thoroughbred Breeders Series

1. New Blood
2. No Hoof, No Horse
3. Recessive
4. Breakover
5. Focus
6. Yearling Sales
7. Grace

Free Rein: New Beginnings

One

Jacqui King let her eyes follow the flight path of a large pelican as it soared above their car, seemingly oblivious to the vehicles below it. She smiled at the sight. The ten year old was excited. This was dampened only as her older brother once again spoke negatively about their current situation.

"I don't understand why we had to move from the country in one state just so that we could spend time in the country in another state. Seriously dad, couldn't you have not accepted the transfer at work?" Ross King asked for what felt like the millionth time to Jacqui.

The family of four had been on the road for around 10 hours, travelling interstate to their new home.

Jacqui's father had been offered a position at work that had excited both of her parents. Unfortunately it had meant moving interstate halfway through the year and leaving behind many family members and friends.

Jacqui's apprehension had been made smaller when her mother had talked of the 100 acre property that they would be leasing in Victoria. Her excitement had grown further still when she was told that the property used to be set up for agistment and it was Kate's hope – Jacqui's mother – that this would be a future possibility for the whole family. After all, a large property would be expensive and needed justification by earning its keep, Jacqui had been told.

From a young age Jacqui had dreamt of horses. Whilst living in the country in South Australia with her family, she had had opportunities to be led on friends' ponies but that was all. It seemed that only now would Jacqui be able to pursue her ultimate dream of having her own horse – and on their property!

Tuning out her brother's ongoing list of complaints about their move, Jacqui took in the houses and land that they drove past, hoping theirs looked as wonderful. Large brick homes stood behind well manicured green lawns, roses lining driveways in full bloom. *It looks so wonderful.*

Half an hour later the Kings made their way down a dead end street, Kate excitedly telling Jacqui that their property was at the end of this road. Jacqui sat up taller in the back seat, eager to see their property as soon as she could. She chanced a glance in her brother's direction, noting sadly that he had his eyes closed and the earphones of his ipod in place.

"Here we are!" Kate breathed out excitedly, opening her door as Tony put the car into park.

Accepting a key that her husband handed her, Kate made her way quickly to the gate that was pulled shut over the driveway, a large padlock keeping it closed. An old wooden sign half hung from the gate, the name of the property on it in faded white paint. *Genesis.* Jacqui smiled as it seemed that her mother almost skipped in her excitement.

The padlock was unlocked quickly and Kate got back into the car. Tony drove down the curved driveway, heading for where he knew the house was.

Jacqui didn't notice the lack of carefully manicured lawns or roses lining the drive in bloom. She was too in awe of the large open paddocks that seemed to go on and on. *Just how big is 100 acres?* She grinned, already picturing herself racing across them on a little grey pony. *This is going to be great!*

Ross awoke in time to race his sister into the house, claiming the largest of the three available bedrooms for either of them. Kate and Tony had taken the main bedroom close to the front door. Jacqui chose the smallest of the three rooms left, concluding that a smaller space of her own meant less she would have to keep clean.

She placed her suitcase on the bed that had already been made up by their mother a few days prior.

Once things had been confirmed with Tony's job and then with this property, Kate had flown over to Victoria for a day to clean up the dusty old house. She'd also made an extra effort to make the bedrooms ready for her two children. Jacqui hadn't liked her mother being away for a night but that was over and done with now.

She opened up the curtains that covered the one window in her room and looked out over two large paddocks that were behind the house. *This place really is huge!* Glancing back at her bed, Jacqui grinned.

She ran to the end of it and sat back to face the window, swinging her legs happily. *And I can see right out of the window onto paddocks that will have horses in them – all from my bed!*

As far as the ten year old was concerned at this very moment, things were perfect.

Geordie Smith worked the curry comb in circular motions, eager to get all of the sweat out of her mount's body. Where the girth had lain and up over the pony's shoulders there were patches of sweat.

"Hannah, can you hand me a body brush?" she asked of her 10 year old best friend.

Glancing around, Hannah realised that their instructor Emmy was focused on a figure headed their way. Quickly Hannah picked up the body brush from a big pile of brushes in the middle of their tie up area.

She threw it toward Geordie, cringing when her friend's pony Sheila shied at the sudden object flying toward her.

"Hannah! Why did you throw that to me and scare Sheila? I'm glad I finished riding her before you scared her!"

"Sorry," Hannah replied meekly, putting her body brush back in the bucket.

"I didn't think it would scare her. I'll remember not to throw things around the horses."

The figure Emmy had been watching was Geordie's older brother Johnny. He greeted the red head with a smile and hello before asking the two girls how their lesson had been.

"Great as per usual!" Hannah replied, Geordie nodding enthusiastically.

4

"I jumped 45 centimetres today, Johnny! Maybe next time we come for our lesson you could stay and watch us?"

The older male smiled, saying that he might just do that.

"Are you two ready? I promised Hannah's mother that I'd have her home before six."

"Nearly! Emmy, can you help me with this rug?" Hannah questioned, struggling to pull the heavy material down from the rail it was hanging over.

Their instructor came to her aid quickly, placing it over Dundee's body after checking that Hannah had attacked all the sweaty areas of the dun pony. She let Hannah buckle up the straps, reminding her to do the hind leg straps first, then the front and finally the two belly straps that crisscrossed over each other.

"Are you ok, Geordie?" Johnny asked, watching his younger sister stare at her pony, deep in thought.

"Why doesn't Sheila have a rug, Emmy?"

"She actually does, Geordie! Unfortunately one of the other ponies must have had a disagreement with Sheila. This morning we found her rug with two large holes and barely hanging on. We've had to put it in the repair pile and my mother has put in an order for a new one. When the new rug comes, we'll put that on Sheila."

"But won't she get cold?"

"Horses generally prefer it to be cold, rather than hot. She won't get too cold and they can survive without rugs on. We tend to put them on the horses here so that you who ride them don't have to spend all of your time brushing out mud before a saddle can be put on!"

"I like that idea," Hannah stated with a smile, undoing the quick release knot that had been used to tie Dundee up to a post.

Geordie wasn't so sure, thinking that the horse's comfort was more important than whether she needed to brush out mud or not.

"Could I bring Sheila a rug to wear?" she asked her instructor.

"That's such a wonderful offer, Geordie. I promise you we'll have one for Sheila to wear by tomorrow though. Perhaps you can start saving for a rug for when you get your own pony?"

Liking the sound of that idea, Geordie also undid her mount and walked with Hannah out to the pony paddock where they were kept. Emmy and Johnny followed close behind.

Jacqui took her mother's hand in her left, her father's in her right. The King family were praying together the night before Tony was due to start his new position. It was a tradition of theirs to pray before any big event.

Jacqui closed her eyes as her mother asked God to guide her father in his new position, to aid him in developing right relationships with new colleagues and to be respectful to all and efficient in his work. Jacqui agreed with an amen at the end of the prayer, noting that Ross also said this, although very quietly.

Ross had been quiet all evening, his earphones in over dinner and afterward in their new lounge room. It was only as Kate removed them from Ross' ears and announced that they were going to pray before going to bed that he had grudgingly left them out.

Jacqui anticipated that they would be seeking God's favour together in less than two weeks when they were due at a new school for the second semester. She was more than happy to think about this later however, excited to think about what she could do over the next week and a half with her mother. Kate had already invited her daughter to help her start and establish a veggie garden, to check out the fencing of the property, water sources and to decide on where they could put in a future arena and set of stables.

Jacqui thought about all of these exciting things as she got herself ready for bed, said goodnight to her parents and settled in under the covers in her new room. She made a note to write a letter to Josie, her close friend back in South Australia. She definitely needed to tell her all about the new property that her parents had taken on – but first she would need to check out the property.

Being winter, it had grown dark shortly after they'd arrived at Genesis. Jacqui smiled as she remembered her mother's comment regarding the property's name.

"We'll have to clean up the sign on the front gate, repaint and rehang it. Genesis is so fitting with our new beginning, don't you think?"

Jacqui had agreed. She'd been taught that the first book in the bible named Genesis was the beginning of the world. *And this Genesis will be our beginning.* Having been up since five that morning when they'd had to hit the road,

Jacqui easily fell asleep, dreaming of a perfect little grey pony trotting across the acres of Genesis whilst she sat proudly on top.

Two

Jacqui opened her eyes and stared at the ceiling, listening to the raised voices in the house.

"Would you give this a chance, Ross? Your father's job is very important and it's a great opportunity we've been given with this transfer. It'll work out alright."

"But I don't want to be here! I've left behind all of my friends and now I'll be the new kid in the middle of the year. Everyone at school will have already established their friend groups. Why should they include me?"

"Why shouldn't they? We can pray about this together."

"Like we prayed about dad's job last night?" Ross asked sarcastically.

"Yes. Let's do it now," Kate instructed her son, reaching for his hand.

"No! If God listened to my prayers then we wouldn't even be here! We'd still be home!" he threw back at her angrily.

"Sometimes what we ask for isn't answered as soon as we ask it, nor in a way that we expect, Ross. But that doesn't mean that that's a bad thing," his mother replied, her tone softening.

"It sure seems pretty bad to me!" Ross replied, stalking out of the room and closing the front door with a bang after him.

Jacqui frowned, not liking the way her brother was talking to their mum. Suddenly she jumped out of bed, questioning if she'd slept away much of the day when she should be exploring.

She dressed quickly and met her mother in the kitchen, accepting the bowl of cereal that was offered to her with a smile.

"How did you sleep, honey?"

"Great! Mum… do you think Ross will come to like being here?"

Kate smiled as she paused from writing a list of things to do.

"I sure hope so. He's hurting and scared at the moment. I think things will improve when he's able to establish some friends at school."

"That's a little while away."

""That's true. Perhaps I can find a nearby soccer club that he can join. Maybe that'll cheer him up."

Jacqui nodded.

"What are you writing?"

Kate smiled.

"Our list of things to do! I've got short term, medium and long term items for us to consider. Perhaps when you're out exploring today you'd like to take a pen and paper with you. That way as you think of things, you can write them down and bring them back to me."

Jacqui grinned.

"Awesome! Have you got the veggie garden, stables and arena on the list?"

Kate laughed.

"Definitely. Plus to check the fencing, water and any major hazards in the paddocks. Perhaps you can do some of that today Jacqui as you're out walking. It rained earlier yesterday and the day before according to the weather forecasts so I'm hoping that'll have made some of the soil out the back of the house nice and soft for a veggie patch. I'll start working on that today."

Jacqui hurriedly finished her breakfast, keen to see all of the property that morning. It was half past eight already and her mother had told her that rain was forecast for the afternoon – she needed to get moving!

Pulling on a jacket and a pair of gumboots she stepped off the front porch, running to the back of the house. Here were the two paddocks she'd looked out at through her bedroom window. She unlocked the large gate into the first paddock, being sure to lock it after her in spite of there being no horses on the property.

Jacqui dodged puddles as she walked the perimeter of the paddock, looking at the fences. She patted the pen and paper in her jacket pocket, making sure that they were where she'd put them. The fencing looked old but ok to her,

11

but she wasn't sure what horse fencing should look like. She made a note to ask her mother if she knew.

Jacqui made it to the end of the first paddock and decided to go through the gate into the second. She wanted to turn right and continue around the perimeter of this first paddock she'd entered, but to the left of the next paddock in front of her it looked like there was an arena of sorts and a few figures riding horses.

Curious, she climbed over a small hill that was made up of a large concrete pipe covered over with soil. Water trickled through the pipe and into a large ditch that lined the paddock fence. Jacqui made a note on her piece of paper to tell her mum about it later.

She left the gate open to this second paddock, wanting to get closer to the arena quickly. She grinned as she watched three people riding their horses around an arena at the trot, being instructed by another figure standing in the middle of them.

A horse riding school? We live next to a horse riding school!

Jacqui ran closer, standing at the fence line to watch the three moving across the middle of the arena and then changing direction.

"Don't forget to change your diagonal as you change direction!" their instructor called out, correcting one rider.

Jacqui looked at the three horses, two brown in colour and one a reddish colour. This she knew to be chestnut because of her mother's gift of a horse book a year ago. The horses looked so lovely to Jacqui that she lost track of time watching them. She sighed when the lesson seemed to come to an end, the instructor letting the group of three out of the arena where they disappeared from view.

Jacqui watched for awhile longer but it seemed that no one else was coming to ride in the arena for her to watch. Shrugging her shoulders she continued on down the fence line, knowing that this paddock was the end of their property in one direction.

An hour later she'd walked the perimeters of both paddocks behind the house which made up almost half of the property. There were two other large paddocks – one to the left of the house and another in front, as well as a smaller paddock on the left as you first came down the driveway. There was a gate from the first paddock behind the house into the one that was off to the side of the house and Jacqui used this to start her walk around the outside of the third paddock.

So far she'd found a couple of fence wires down, a big hole in the second paddock and made note of two large areas of water that may be ok for horses to drink from. A wind had picked up halfway around the second paddock and Jacqui realised that apart from her coat, there wasn't much protection from the wind or rain. She wondered how long it'd take trees to grow if she and her mother planted them in groups in all of the paddocks.

She also wondered where her brother had gone. Jacqui knew Ross wouldn't confide in her and felt sad that her brother would be alone while he was upset. She loved this new property and enjoyed spending time with her mother. She knew that for herself, the term holidays would end too quickly and she'd be due back at school.

Later that afternoon her mother was due to take her shopping for the novel that Kate had learnt was to be studied in English for Jacqui's grade five class. Jacqui was fairly sure that her mother would have found out about Ross' school requirements too, but doubted her brother would make use of the holidays to get ahead in school.

The idea didn't appeal much to Jacqui either, but she knew that it wouldn't be a nice feeling to not know what was being discussed in class – especially in a new school. She made a plan to start the book that night if they managed to find a copy to buy.

Hannah Johnston grinned as she picked up the phone. Her mother had told her Geordie was on the line.

"Hello?"

"Hannah! So I got my mum to ask at the East Riding School if they do pony parties, but they said they don't," Geordie informed her best friend.

"Oh! I was so looking forward to us getting to ride all day for your birthday. Now what will we do?" Hannah asked, disappointed.

"I didn't finish! The ERS doesn't, but they told us of a place down the road that does so my mum called them next."

Hannah waited silently on the line. She frowned when Geordie didn't continue.

"And?!"

Geordie laughed.

"I was waiting for you to interrupt me again! And they are free the first weekend in August so my mum's booked! Now we need to work out who else to invite. Apparently they can cater for up to 10 people but they only have five ponies so we'd have to take turns. I think if we only invite three other people, then we can spend the whole time riding!"

Hannah grinned, thinking this a brilliant idea.

"So are you thinking of Amelia and Caitlin from school?" she asked.

"Yup! I just don't know who the third person should be."

"We'll have to think about that. This is going to be so much fun!"

Geordie agreed talking with Hannah about the different games they would get to play on horseback. She concluded this was going to be the best birthday party ever.

The girls decided that planning the pony party made up for the fact that they didn't have another riding lesson until the school term started back. At least school starting up again meant they were a lot closer to going on another ride.

Three

Jacqui watched out of the car window as her brother headed up the steps of his high school quickly. Kate had allowed him to enter the school by himself, not wanting to embarrass her son and because he'd insisted on doing so. Jacqui had noted with relief that over the rest of the school holidays, Ross had stayed quiet around the house but seemed happier, less likely to snap at his mother or father.

She wondered what had caused him to cheer up but decided it didn't matter, as long as he was happier.

She jumped as her mother pulled away from the kerb, rejoining the traffic as they headed off to her new school. Jacqui was nervous. She wondered what type of classmates she'd have and if they'd be nice to the new girl.

All too quickly they arrived at St. James Primary School. Jacqui stepped out of the car with her mother, pulling her backpack closer over her left shoulder. She followed her mum quickly to the front office.

They were directed by an older woman with curly grey hair and glasses to take a left out of the office, travel down to room 11 and introduce themselves to Mr. O'Laughlin.

Jacqui stood awkwardly in the doorway as her mother knocked and gained the teacher's attention. A gentleman she presumed to be Mr. O'Laughlin ushered them in, a few students brushing past them in the doorway. Jacqui looked around the classroom while her mother talked with her teacher. Her eyes were drawn to a drawing of a pony running along the beach, its mane and tail flowing out in the wind behind it. *That's so cool. I wonder who drew it.*

"Welcome to St. James, Jacqui. Have you started the novel that we'll be studying this term?" Mr. O'Laughlin asked her, drawing her gaze from the picture on the wall.

"Yes sir. I've almost finished it," she replied, blushing.

"Great! Why don't you take a seat as we'll get started in a few minutes."

Kate waved goodbye to her daughter with an encouraging smile before she left the room. Jacqui looked at the tables set up to seat four people. She spied a group of three girls talking earnestly and considered joining them.

A backpack placed on the spare chair made her question if it was being saved for someone.

Turning toward another table that was empty she pulled out a chair and sat down. Keen to not look as awkward as she felt, she opened up her bag and started pulling out things she thought she'd need for class. She wrote her name down on the exercise book before going back to looking around the class.

A boy and girl sat opposite her, engaged in a debate. Jacqui decided not to say hello and interrupt them. Another girl sat beside her, pulling out a novel. Jacqui sighed. *This is going to be hard.*

She gave her attention to Mr. O'Laughlin as he welcomed the class back for their third term of school. Jacqui cringed as he also made everyone say hello to her because she was new. She was glad that he hadn't asked her to stand up and tell the class about herself – that would have been embarrassing!

The morning progressed into discussing their study book for that term and reading a chapter from the book. Jacqui had already read that part of the novel and found her attention drawn to one of the three girls she'd originally considered sitting with. The young brown haired figure was drawing quickly across a piece of paper with her left hand, her right holding up the book they were supposed to be reading. Jacqui smiled as she saw the drawing taking the shape of a pony. *I wonder if she drew the picture up on the classroom wall?*

Jacqui felt a pair of eyes on her and looked toward the teacher subconsciously. Mr. O'Laughlin had paused from reading but launched into another paragraph. Jacqui sighed in relief.

She looked back to the table of girls and found one looking at her with a smile on her face. Jacqui returned the smile shyly, returning her attention to the book in front of her.

Shortly after their teacher finished reading the chapter and told the class to write a page about their feelings on the main character. He suggested they include whether they liked the character, why or why not, if they could relate to the main character and would they have made the choice that he did at the end of the chapter?

Jacqui smiled at the easy task they were set. She was glad to find that this class for the time being seemed easy enough for her. She finished writing her page as the bell went, announcing morning tea time.

Slowly she piled her books together on the table, unsure if she should be packing them up.

"We'll be in this classroom again after break," the girl who had smiled at her said, "so you might as well leave your things."

"Ok," Jacqui responded, pulling out an apple and a drink.

"Do you like horses?" the same girl asked, looking at Jacqui expectantly.

She glanced at her three friends leaving the classroom before looking back to Jacqui, awaiting a reply.

"Umm… yeah… why?"

"I saw you looking at Hannah's drawing. She did the one on the classroom wall, too," she informed Jacqui, pointing up to the picture of the horse on the beach that she'd been admiring earlier.

"Do you like it?"

"It's great," Jacqui replied honestly, following the girl as she headed out of the classroom after her friends.

"Come meet the others," the girl instructed, jogging across the school grounds.

Jacqui ran to keep up with her. She wondered if she would find out this girl's name.

"I'm Jacqui," she stated, a bit unsure.

"I know. Mr O'Laughlin did introduce you," she replied with a smile as they stopped at her group of friends.

"Perhaps she was telling you that Geordie in the hope that you'd provide your name," Hannah replied with a smirk.

Geordie blushed.

"Oh. Sorry Jacqui."

Hannah laughed.

"I'm Hannah and this is Caitlin and Amelia," Hannah introduced the three friends Geordie had led her to.

Jacqui said hello and sat down cross legged to join them. The girls were talking about the book Mr. O'Laughlin had been reading in class.

"It's so boring!" Amelia sighed, pulling at some grass on the school oval that they were sitting on.

"You'll like the ending," Hannah replied with a grin.

"Do you have to rub it in that you've already finished it?" Amelia asked with a frown, and then, "have you started it yet, Jacqui?"

Jacqui blushed; not wanting to say that she'd almost finished the book and was really enjoying it.

"Yeah," she responded simply.

"So Jacqui likes horses," Geordie mentioned suddenly, drawing the three other girl's eyes to her immediately.

"Is... that a bad thing?" Jacqui asked uncertainly.

"Not at all!" Geordie replied with a grin, "we love them! Well, Hannah and I do."

"Hey! Just because we don't spend every second obsessing about our dream pony doesn't mean that we don't like them," Amelia cut in, Caitlin nodding in agreement.

"Exactly. But there are other things to life outside of horses. So what did you guys do over the school holidays?"

"Read the English book and horse rode," Hannah replied simply, causing Jacqui to giggle.

"What about you, Jacqui?" Caitlin asked pointedly, turning her back to Geordie and Hannah.

"Well… my family just moved here from South Australia. So we were unpacking in our new house and getting things organised for going to a new school… that's about it."

Caitlin nodded, asking Jacqui about why her family moved. The five girls chattered until the bell went for them to return to class. Hannah sighed, questioning out loud if they would have to deal with Mr. O'Laughlin reading another chapter from their English text. Geordie laughed, reminding her that if he did, that'd just give her more time to draw horse pictures. This cheered her up immediately.

Jacqui was glad to find her mother waiting in their car outside the school as soon as she was finished. She raced to the passenger side, pausing as she opened up the back door.

"Where's Ross?"

"Home already," Kate replied with a smile, "he finishes earlier than you and asked me if he could catch the bus home."

Jacqui nodded, closing the back door and instead sitting in the front beside her mum.

"So, what's the verdict?" Kate asked, glancing at her daughter with a smile before focusing on driving the car home.

"Ok, I think! Class seemed fairly straight forward and I met four girls who all like horses. One of them can draw *really* well. It'll be nice to have some new friends," Jacqui commented, causing Kate to smile again.

"That's great, honey. I'm glad God provided you with some people with similar interests on your first day! I've got a surprise for you when we get home."

"For me?"

"Well, for all of us. Ross knows what it is already."

Jacqui sat quietly, questioning what on earth it could be. *A pony?* She grinned at the thought but considered that to be very unlikely. *So what is it?*

She chattered with her mum the short drive home, forgetting about the surprise as she detailed the three teacher's she'd met that day. She mentioned to her mother that so far she liked Mr. O'Laughlin the best.

"I wonder if you'll have any new teachers tomorrow," Kate mused, pausing to let her daughter enter the house first.

Jacqui squealed in delight as a young dog jumped up at her when she came through the front door.

"Mum! He's gorgeous! Have you named him? What does Ross think? …does dad know?!"

Kate laughed.

"Ross has named him Jack and has already volunteered to take him out each day for a walk. Your father... will find out when he gets home," she answered, causing Jacqui to laugh.

"I can't believe you bought a dog without checking with dad! Jack! Jack! We're going to have so much fun!" she stated excitedly, skipping around the house, the young kelpie jumping and running with her.

"If you put a leash on him Jacqui, perhaps you can help him to burn off some excess energy," Kate suggested, eyeing some china wear in the lounge with concern.

Jacqui agreed, taking the leash offered to her.

"Come on boy, let's go for a walk!"

The young kelpie trotted happily by her side but Jacqui didn't dare take the lead off in case he decided to explore further than she was ready to. Beside, two boundaries of their property were lined by roads, on a freeway. That wasn't a place for a young dog.

Tuesday afternoon found Geordie and Hannah back at the East Riding School for their much anticipated horse riding lesson.

"Eyes up, Geordie! Remember, if you look down at the jump-"

"That's where you'll end up!" Geordie finished for Emmy, her horse riding instructor as she focused beyond the crossbar she was taking Sheila over.

She managed this successfully, asking her pony to come back to a walk as she'd be instructed to before heading

23

into the centre of the arena to let Hannah try out the small course of three jumps on Dundee.

"Well done! You're improving fast, Geordie. We just need to keep your focus beyond the jump!"

Geordie grinned at the praise.

"Thanks!"

She watched Hannah push Dundee out into a trot, rising to the outside foreleg as she'd been taught to do. Geordie knew that they had to follow a particular leg diagonal to rise and fall to so that the horse travelled more easily and in balance. She loved everything that they learnt as well as what they got to do when horse riding.

Hannah completed the small course twice as Geordie had done, fixing up a couple of inconsistencies that Emmy pointed out to her as she rode. Then she joined her friend in the middle, looking down at Emmy standing before them.

"Ok, who's up for a race?" Emmy questioned, grinning as both girls nodded vigorously.

"I'm going to time you each going through the course twice. Things we don't want to forget about as we try to do the course fast are heading for the middle of the jump, our trotting diagonal and rising into our 2 point position over the jump. Any questions?"

Both girls shook their head no. Emmy smiled.

"Who's first?"

Geordie threw her hand up quickly, grinning when she realised she'd just beat Hannah.

"Ok Geordie, I want you to warm up Sheila at a trot and when you pass the letter A, I'll start timing. Good luck!"

Geordie pushed her mount into a walk and then a trot, checking her diagonal as she headed toward the letter A at one end of the arena. She made sure that her heels were down, her toes up and her hands sitting lightly above her horse's wither as she headed towards the first jump.

They rose over this, then took the second and third just as neatly. Geordie grinned, thinking it time to push Sheila out a little bit faster. She applied more pressure with her leg, rising a little higher in the saddle for each trot stride.

Sheila responded, lengthening her stride and therefore covering ground a little quicker, giving Geordie her desired result. Geordie was grinning from ear to ear as she finished the last jump and brought Sheila back to a swinging walk.

"That felt awesome!"

Emmy laughed in delight.

"You looked great! And I'm glad to see your focus stayed beyond each jump – well done! Hannah, you're up!"

Geordie was still grinning as she watched her friend go through the course. She concluded after one lap of the jumps that Hannah was moving faster than she had, but she seemed to be focused more on her speed than hitting the centre of each jump, Geordie thought. She made a note to tell Hannah so.

Both girls managed a clear round, their ponies capably jumping the small course asked of them. Emmy congratulated both on achieving this small task.

"So – who won?" Hannah asked breathlessly as she trotted over to the pair, remembering to bring Dundee back to a walk before she got too close.

"I think you both did," Emmy responded, "Geordie your course looked so stylish and you managed the second round faster than the first. And Hannah you cleared all of the jumps well and kept up a fast past the whole way around."

"Yes, but who was faster?" Hannah pushed, a knowing smile on her face.

"You were," Emmy laughed, catching the competitive tone in her client's voice.

"But like I said, I think you're both winners. How about I let you out of the arena so you can do a lap and cool your ponies down before you untack and brush them over?"

"Ha! Beat you!" Hannah stated with cheer, holding onto the buckle of her reins as Dundee lengthened her neck and headed after their instructor.

"You were faster, that's true," Geordie responded, thinking that accuracy and style were more important than speed.

"So I was thinking of asking Jacqui if she'd like to come to my pony party next month," Geordie suggested, walking Shelia behind Hannah and Dundee.

Hannah turned around to face her friend, letting her pony continue on the familiar routine.

"Do you even know if she rides?"

"Not yet. But she likes horses. What do you think?"

Hannah shrugged.

"I guess… you were looking for a fifth person to come along. Why not?"

Geordie grinned.

"Great. I'll ask her at school tomorrow."

Four

Geordie let out a relieved sigh as the bell went for morning tea.

"Finally!"

The girls made their way out of the classroom, Jacqui glad that for the past couple of days she'd been able to sit with them over break and lunch. Today was no exception.

"So I wanted to ask you something," Geordie grinned, catching Jacqui's gaze.

She paused from chewing on her apple, uncertain.

"Yeah?"

"Next weekend we're celebrating my birthday with a pony party. Did you want to come?"

"It's your birthday next weekend? Happy birthday for then!" Jacqui responded with a smile.

"Well actually it's the following Monday, but any excuse to ride horses on the weekend is good for me! So, will you come?"

"So the pony party will include riding the horses?" Jacqui asked, uncertain about her first time not being led on a horse being in front of her new school friends.

"Of course! We'll get to play games on horseback and there's enough horses for each person to get their own. You won't have to hop off at all!" Geordie stated with a triumphant grin.

Jacqui smiled meekly.

"I might have to ask my mum about it..."

"Ok. Let me know tomorrow," Geordie replied simply.

"Ok," Jacqui agreed, munching on her apple while thinking.

How can I learn to ride a horse before two weekends time? She was pretty sure she should just say no to the invitation to avoid embarrassment, but was happy to have bought some time to think about it.

Geordie and Hannah started discussing their horse riding lesson from the night before.

"Do all of you guys ride often?" Jacqui asked, curious.

"Amelia and I do every now and again, but it's really expensive so our parents let us go on trail rides instead. That way we pay the same amount, but we get to ride longer," Caitlin explained with a smile.

"And you two?" Jacqui asked Hannah and Geordie.

"All the time!" Geordie replied enthusiastically.

"She means once a fortnight," Hannah corrected with a smile.

"Our parents also agree that it's a lot to pay for, but during the school term we get to go every second Tuesday night and have a lesson together. It's cheaper than a private lesson," she stated simply.

Jacqui guessed a private lesson was one where you rode by yourself but she was too shy to check. Geordie and Hannah went back to discussing the jumping course they'd done in their lesson, arguing over who had been better.

Jacqui thought it must be a wonderful feeling to jump a horse as fast as you could, while still showing style and grace. She couldn't wait to learn to ride.

"What did you get for question five?" Geordie whispered to Hannah as they sat in their math class.

Hannah sighed.

"I'm up to question three. Why don't you ask Amelia?"

Geordie looked to the two opposite her. They were focused on their tests. Geordie sighed and continued working through the questions. She really liked math, but liked to check that others had gotten the same answers as her. She finished well before the other three and found herself daydreaming about their last horse riding lesson.

Hannah may have indeed been the fastest, but Geordie felt it was more important to do things correctly than quickly. She couldn't wait until she had a pony of her own to ride around a jumping course and enter into shows. She'd talked with her parents about owning a horse but they'd said at the moment that a pony would cost too much to buy.

Geordie sadly recognised that even if she did have enough to buy a pony at that stage, there would be the costs of keeping it somewhere and looking after its health, too.

Suddenly she wished that she was turning 15 instead of 11, then she could get a job to help pay for it. *I hope I get a pony before I turn 15!*

"Mum, we're home!" Jacqui called out as she entered the house and dumped her bag at the door.

Ross had agreed to try out catching the bus to Jacqui's school that day in time to pick her up at the end of her day. Then they'd travelled home together. Kate had been applying for part time jobs and pointed out to her son that if she ended up working afternoons, then she needed to know that her children were getting home safely.

"Bags in your room!" Kate called out from the kitchen.

Jacqui smiled, picking her bag back up from the hallway and taking it to her room. She decided she should change before heading out to check on the veggie garden her mum had been working on.

Ross dumped his bag in his room and emerged shortly after, in warmer clothes and out of his uniform.

"I'm taking Jack for a walk!" he called out, closing the door behind him shortly after.

Jack had met the pair excitedly at the front door of the house. Tony had accepted their new pet, but had insisted that a dog's place was outside, not in the house. He'd put together a dog house from some wooden pallets that had been left on the property by the previous occupants.

31

"Did you get some new plants for the veggie garden?" Jacqui asked her mum, entering the kitchen.

"I did! And some seeds too. Now we have broccoli, beans, peas and some berry plants in. It'll look great when spring comes around. How was your day?"

"Pretty good... I got invited to a birthday party next weekend."

"That's great! I guess we'd better go present shopping this weekend. What does she like?"

"Horses," Jacqui responded without having to think.

"I told them I'd have to ask you about going..."

"Are you not sure about going to the party?"

"It sounds wonderful mum... but I'm afraid I'll just embarrass myself and get the other girls frustrated with me."

"Why is that?" Kate asked, sitting down at the dining table opposite her daughter.

"Apparently it's a pony party. Geordie said everyone would have their own pony to ride for the party and that that means we would get to stay on the ponies for the whole time. I asked them how often they rode horses and Geordie and Hannah said that they have a riding lesson every two weeks after school on a Tuesday. Today they were talking about a jumping course that they did yesterday in their lesson!"

"And the other girls?" Kate asked with an understanding smile.

"Apparently they go on trail rides as often as they can. Their parents say that lessons are too expensive, but they said they can ride for longer on a trail ride, but for the same price as a lesson. It sounds like they've ridden a lot too."

"Did you ask them how long they've been riding for?" Kate asked gently.

"No mum… but if they're doing jumping courses then I really do think that they won't like that I don't even know how to trot on a horse yet. I think I should tell them no."

"I can understand why you feel that way. So how will you tell them?"

"Perhaps I could tell them that my parents don't want me to go?" Jacqui asked hopefully.

Kate smiled.

"I'm sorry Jacqui, but that would be lying. If these girls are your friends, you should tell them the truth and they should accept it. Perhaps you can say that you'd love to go to the party but you don't have any horse riding experience yet and you don't want to slow down their fun."

Jacqui sighed.

"I guess so."

"It'll be ok honey. Try not to worry about something that you can't do anything about until tomorrow. Why don't you enjoy some time outside while the sun's out? Don't forget your coat though, it's cold out there! I've still got some seeds to plant in the garden if you'd like to help me with that?" Kate offered.

"Thanks mum. I might go for a walk."

"Ok."

Jacqui grabbed her jacket and made her way outside. She headed to the largest paddock on the property that was lined by the freeway on one side. The wind grabbed at her and she remembered that she wanted to talk with her mum about creating more wind protection in the paddocks if they were eventually to have a lot of horses on the property.

Kate had been doing some research and was keen to offer agistment in the near future. She'd already fixed up the fencing issues that Jacqui had found and made sure that water was available in each paddock, and that the gates were in working order.

Jacqui thought about how she was going to tell Geordie that she didn't want to go to the party. She smiled as she saw Ross and Jack walking toward her. Ross bent down and must have unclipped the leash because suddenly Jack was racing toward her. Jacqui laughed as the young kelpie jumped up against her legs, reaching up to lick her face.

"Hello Jack! I'm glad you ran to me once Ross let you off the lead!"

She played with the pup until her brother caught up with them.

"I wasn't sure if he'd come straight to you, but I hoped," Ross commented, patting Jack on the head and clipping him up again.

"I'm glad he did! I don't think mum would be happy if he ended up loose and lost."

"I'm sure she wouldn't be. Did she say if we would be catching the bus home again tomorrow?" he asked.

"No. But I think we will again."

Ross nodded before saying that he was heading back to the house. Jacqui watched him walk off before continuing on the way she wanted to go.

Jacqui was surprised to spot a figure riding by themselves in the paddock next door to their property. She grinned as she questioned if all of their neighbours had horses and rode.

They had one neighbour next to them where their property was the end of their street, and another in the form of the riding school. Now it seemed that on the other side of their property, was someone else who had at least one horse. That left one other property that sat beside theirs that Jacqui didn't know about.

She increased her pace, eager to get a closer look at the horse and rider.

Again Jacqui found herself paused at a boundary fence line of their property, watching someone else ride. From what she could see, the rider was female and looked to be about Ross' age. Jacqui smiled as she watched the girl go from a trot into a canter and continue on a circle.

She was surprised to note that this girl was riding in an open paddock. *But where's the arena?*

Jacqui contemplated running away when the girl spotted her and waved from the back of her horse as she came trotting over. She stayed at the fence line, unsure.

"Hi! I guess you're one of my new neighbours!" she stated with a smile, putting Jacqui at ease.

"Hi. I guess so. I'm Jacqui King."

"I'm Kara. So I guess you're Ross' younger sister then?"

Jacqui frowned. *How does she know Ross?*

"Uh… yeah."

"I met Ross a couple of weeks ago when I was out riding Banjo here. He mentioned he had a younger sister who loves horses. I was hoping I'd get to meet you sooner!"

Jacqui smiled.

"I love them, but I have no idea how to ride," she found herself blurting out, blushing.

"That's how we all start!"

"I guess so… I'm just not sure when I'll get to start. Mum dreams of us turning this place into an agistment property for horses but we don't have any stables, an arena to ride in and I definitely don't have a pony to ride!"

"That last one makes it very difficult," Kara said with a smile, "but stables aren't important. Banjo here has a shelter that he uses if it's really windy or raining and we ride in this paddock. I keep him in the one next door," she pointed back over her shoulder as she explained to Jacqui.

"So if you ride in the paddock, how do you keep Banjo in the area you want to ride him in? Don't things get out of control?"

"Not with Banjo!" Kara replied, patting her gelding on the neck.

"Mum and dad made sure they bought me a horse that was really quiet. He's what people often call 'bombproof'. He's a bit older and has been ridden by many people. He's been the best first horse ever."

"When did you get him?" Jacqui asked, reaching over the fence to let him sniff at her hand.

"Last year. I've only had him just over a year," Kara replied with a proud smile.

"And did you ride before that?" Jacqui asked, believing that Kara must have been riding since a very young age.

"Yup! Mum and dad paid for four lessons for me, over a month. Once I could walk, trot and canter, that was it! They told me it was cheaper for me to have a horse that I could practice on at home, rather than have to have lessons each week. They were right. I've learnt so much on Banjo."

"So you've only been riding a year and after four lessons you got a horse?" Jacqui asked, amazed.

Kara laughed.

"Yup! That's what worked for me and my parents, so that's what we did! I don't need a fancy arena to ride in, just a quiet horse and some flat ground. We're learning lots and sometimes mum and dad get an instructor to come out and teach me on Banjo so I have more to work on, but on my own horse at home! It's the best."

Jacqui found herself grinning as she stood there in the cold. *Maybe I can get mum to book me in for some lessons at the riding school next door and then we can go looking for a pony to buy... That would be awesome!*

"So how did you know that Banjo was the right horse to buy?" Jacqui asked, thinking of her dream little grey pony.

"Well he was advertised as quiet, was an older horse that had been ridden for years and I got to test ride him on the day we went to see him and then lease him for a month to make sure that he and I were both happy. It was a great way to do things. So when do you think you'll get to start riding?"

"I'm not sure… there's a riding school next to us that I thought I might be able to talk with mum about… but I've heard that horse riding lessons are expensive."

"They can be! But sometimes they're not at all if you've got a friend who has a horse you can ride," Kara finished with a grin.

Jacqui nodded, agreeing.

"I wish I could say I had that!"

"You do! Me! What about on the weekend? If your parents are happy with it, you can come over and I can lead you around on Banjo. I won't let you loose with him in the paddock; just get you used to steering him and walking and trotting. How does that sound?"

"Are you for real?" Jacqui beamed.

"I am! But maybe I should meet your parents first to make sure they're happy with my suggestion. My parents really don't mind who I put up on Banjo and he's been great with my friends who don't have much riding experience… I'd better keep moving as horses can get cold if they stand around too long and I've already warmed him up. But if you're happy to, meet me here on Saturday morning at around 9 and we'll have a ride!"

Jacqui stared after Kara as she trotted off on her horse. *I have a new friend and I get to ride a horse soon!* She concluded at that second that their move to Victoria was quite possibly the best thing in the world. Jacqui raced across the paddock to tell her mum the good news.

Five

Jacqui had been unsure when her parents had made the walk out with her across the paddock on Saturday morning. Kate had taken her to a nearby saddlery after discussing the option of horse riding with her husband, but Jacqui didn't feel that her new helmet guaranteed that she would be allowed to ride with Kara's help.

What if they don't like the look of Kara and decide she's not responsible enough to lead me around on Banjo? What if they think Banjo's too big to risk riding and possibly falling off?

Her questions were silenced when her mum climbed between the fence wires and encouraged Jacqui to join her as she said hello to Banjo, patting him on the neck. Tony joined them when Kate had finished questioning Kara and seen her take Banjo through a walk and trot around the paddock.

Kate was glowing as she watched her husband give their daughter a boost into the saddle. The pair then stood back as Kara explained to Jacqui about how to hold the reins and where her legs should be. They watched silently as Kara took Banjo for a walk, telling Jacqui how to ask him to turn left and right, how to stop and how to go.

Jacqui didn't notice when her parents made their way back through the fence and went for a walk around the large paddock. She was too busy focusing on how good it felt to be riding a horse!

Kara had informed her that Banjo was 15.2 hands high. Horses were measured in hands which were around ten centimetres each. This meant that Banjo was taller than one and a half metres at his wither – the tallest point at the base of his neck.

Jacqui didn't know much about horse heights, but she was pretty sure that Geordie and Hannah rode ponies. *Wait till I tell them about this at school on Monday!*

She asked Kara what height a pony was, and was amazed to find that they could be as small as 7 hands high, up to just over 14 hands.

"I can't imagine a pony as small as 7 hands!" she stated in wonder, asking Banjo to stop as Kara directed her.

"I know, small isn't it? I've only seen pictures of them. There's a breed called the Falabella and they're that small. They look so cute! So! How do you feel about trying out a trot?"

Jacqui looked unsure.

"But I don't know how to trot," she responded, sitting quietly on Banjo.

"Well how about we go for a walk first with you behaving as if we were trotting?"

"How do you mean?"

"Well, when a horse trots, they move their legs in pairs. This results in the trot feeling bouncy, so to make it appear less bouncy, we rise out of the saddle while one pair moves, and then sit down in the saddle while the other pair moves. This is called rising to the trot."

Jacqui nodded, digesting the information.

"So as Banjo walks, maybe you can just practice standing up and sitting down. But make sure that you don't sit down with a thump. That'll hurt his back," Kara warned, telling Jacqui to ask Banjo to walk on.

Jacqui did so, pleased to find that as she squeezed with her legs, Banjo obediently moved forward.

"Let's just go in a straight line for now. Then you can focus on rising and sitting without having to worry about steering. Does that sound ok?" Kara looked up at Jacqui from where she was walking at Banjo's shoulder.

Jacqui nodded, slowly rising up out of the saddle and sitting down. Kara told her that if she felt she needed to, Jacqui could rest her hands on the front of the saddle.

"Are you taking this all in?" Kara asked with a grin.

"I think so! But I think there's a lot you're not telling me so I don't think it's all too much," she stated shyly, smiling.

Kara laughed.

"Clever girl! Ok, are you ready for a trot?"

Jacqui nodded yes. Kara told Jacqui to squeeze a little more with her legs to tell Banjo to go faster. At the same time she applied pressure to the lead rope she was holding onto, and started jogging beside her gelding.

Banjo picked up a slow trot, Jacqui bouncing a few times before she placed her hands on the front of the saddle to balance herself. She was then able to rise and sit, timing this with Kara as she called out 'up, down, up down.'

Jacqui grinned as Kara pulled Banjo back to a walk, patting him on the neck.

"Good boy!"

Jacqui patted him too.

"Thanks Banjo!" she stated breathlessly.

Kara turned Banjo around so that they were facing back the way they had come.

"Ready to do that again?" she asked with a knowing grin.

Jacqui laughed and nodded. She didn't need asking twice!

Geordie turned her pony around, pushing him into a trot as she ran away from 'the wolf'. She was having a ball at her birthday party.

At this moment one of the girls was 'it', posing as the big bad wolf at one end of the arena they were playing in. The other three started from the far end of the arena and had to call out 'what's the time Mr. Wolf?'

Whatever time the wolf said it was, they had to take this many steps whilst mounted on their horses. When the wolf declared that it was dinner time, all of them – wolf included – had to race as fast as they could on their ponies to the end of the arena. If the wolf beat any of them there, that person was the next wolf.

So far Geordie had managed to not be the wolf, Hannah had been once whilst the other two girls had each had two goes. What helped the girls to focus on their riding was that each time they were able to run away from the wolf, their party organiser had already told them at which pace they were allowed to go.

It had been a challenge for the girls to go as quickly as they could, but keep to a walk and trot. Geordie was glad that for this next round they were allowed to canter away from the wolf. She found that as the wolf declared it was dinner time that her pony didn't want to canter however, and so she was made the wolf for the first time.

"No fair! I couldn't get Matty to canter for me!" she whined, trotting her pony down to the far end to be the wolf.

The other three told her bad luck, glad to see that she finally had to be the one up the front calling out the time. Geordie redeemed herself, managing to beat all three of the girls to the end of the arena as her time of being the wolf. She grinned smugly as she waited for them to catch up.

This game finished, their party instructor told the girls they should cool down their ponies at a walk and then come out of the arena to tie them up and enjoy some food. Geordie grinned, thinking that a brilliant idea. She was getting hungry.

"This has been great so far!" Amelia exclaimed before biting into a party pie.

Caitlin nodded enthusiastically.

"It's a shame that Jacqui couldn't come, but I think she was right in saying no because she hasn't ridden before."

Geordie nodded, thinking that to be true. *But I've got to find a way to help her learn to horse ride. I wonder if she can just ask her parents to get her some riding lessons. Maybe she can eventually join Hannah and I when we ride! That'd make our lessons cheaper, too. Then maybe I could convince mum and dad to put that saved money away for a horse.*

She grinned at the great idea.

"What are you thinking?" Hannah whispered conspiratorially, stepping closer to Geordie.

Geordie laughed.

"I was just wondering if Jacqui's parents would pay for her to have lessons at the East Riding School. Perhaps as she improves, she could join us in our lesson. Then we'd go from a semi-private rate to a group rate. And then," she paused for dramatic effect, "my parents could put away the money they save towards a pony for me!"

Hannah laughed.

"That sounds like the perfect plan. But do you think Jacqui would take long to catch up to us?" she questioned, a tone of superiority in her voice.

Geordie shrugged.

"I don't know. But we can find out sooner if Jacqui starts lessons," she responded decidedly.

The girls enjoyed a half hour break – as did their ponies – before they headed back out to warm them up and take part in a follow the leader trail ride. This time their party instructor was mounted, leading them up and down hills, over small jumps and weaving around barrels. Geordie was exhausted at the end of the day but didn't think that she'd had a better birthday party. What could be better than riding most of the day?

Jacqui grinned as she looked up from her bed to the hook hanging on the back of her bedroom door. Her dad had put it up for her that afternoon so that she had somewhere to hang her helmet out of the way. She was excited to think that she had another lesson with Kara on Sunday afternoon, after the Kings had been to church and had lunch.

Kara had offered to help Jacqui during the week with a lesson every Wednesday, too but Jacqui had declined. It was a habit in the King residence to do school work on week nights before anything else and Jacqui knew that it'd be dark at times before she'd finished.

She knew school was going to get busier and already had her Saturday afternoon planned with working on a project. Sundays were a day to rest and enjoy family time and it was enough for her to know that she got to ride again then.

Jacqui turned her attention back to the horse book her mother had given her. Kate had unpacked all of her books and found an old basic horse care book that she'd had and given it to her daughter. Jacqui had treated the second hand gift like it was an expensive treasure. She decided that on Monday at school she would visit the library and borrow as many horse books as she was allowed to.

Jacqui looked up as someone knocked at her door. She smiled at Ross.

"Come in!"

"How did your ride go?" Ross questioned, sitting on the end of her bed.

Jacqui smiled.

"It was great, Ross! Maybe Kara can teach you to ride, too?" she questioned with a grin, teasing her brother.

Ross blushed.

"I don't think horses are for me, Jacqui. I know you and mum love them, but I think dad and I will stick with the maintenance side of running this property," Ross replied, matter of fact.

"Sounds good to me! So... Kara said to tell you that the movie is on at six tomorrow night and that there's a bus you can catch at five to get there on time... do mum and dad know you have a date?" she asked with a cheeky smile.

Ross grabbed one of Jacqui's pillows, throwing it at her. Jacqui ducked, laughing as Ross headed for the door. He turned back to look at his younger sister.

"Thanks Jaq," he replied with a small smile.

Jacqui just grinned in response. She was glad that Kara seemed to be getting along with Ross and wondered if this was what had caused her brother to cheer up so quickly after their move to Genesis.

Six

Jacqui grinned as she listened to the four girls telling of Geordie's pony party. She laughed a couple of times as they disagreed on the order of events or who had won a particular game.

"It sounds great!" she responded enthusiastically.

"It was!" Hannah agreed.

"But it would have been even cooler if you'd been able to come along and ride with us... so I've got a plan," Geordie stated in a conspiratorial whisper.

Jacqui leaned in closer to Geordie who was sitting next to her on the school oval.

"We thought that you could have a couple of private lessons at the East Riding School and then once you're good enough, you could join us for a group lesson each fortnight!" Geordie finished with a flourish, grinning widely.

Jacqui frowned.

"I thought you guys said that riding lessons were quite expensive... with my dad just starting this new position and mum not having a job yet... I'm not sure," she stated, watching Geordie's face fall, "but I can ask!"

Geordie grinned.

"Great!"

"So… where is the East Riding School?" Jacqui asked, thinking she'd need all the information if she were to ask her parents.

Secretly she preferred the idea of lessons with Kara each week. She knew it was close by, loved Banjo already and thought Kara was a great teacher. Plus, it was free!

"Oh it's not too far from school, maybe about fifteen minutes by car. You live close to this school, don't you?"

Jacqui nodded.

"It's on Rivers Road in Barwon," she added as an afterthought.

Rivers road! That's the road that one side of our property is on! Jacqui laughed as she realised that they had lessons at the riding school next door to her. *How cool is that!*

Hannah frowned.

"What's so funny?"

Jacqui laughed harder.

"I think I should come along and watch you guys ride! When's your next lesson?"

"Tuesday next week," Geordie responded.

"Why?" Hannah asked suspiciously.

Amelia and Caitlin looked on in interest. Jacqui suddenly felt shy under their scrutinizing gaze.

"Umm… would you believe that… I live next door to your riding school?"

"What?!" Geordie and Hannah asked at the same time.

"I guess I haven't told you guys... but when we moved over here from South Australia, mum and dad found a property they could lease... one side of our property touches Rivers Road... but technically we live on Penny Boulevard."

The four girls sat quietly, digesting this new piece of information.

"So... what do you guys do with the property?" Caitlin asked, curious.

"Well... nothing yet. Actually... mum's got this dream of turning it into an agistment property but at the moment it needs a lot of work. Fences need to be better, shelters put in, more trees..." Jacqui started listing the items.

"Agistment?" Amelia asked, unfamiliar with the word.

Geordie squealed, gaining everyone's attention.

"This... is brilliant! Jacqui, how big is the property?"

Jacqui blushed.

"Umm... 100 acres?"

Geordie jumped to her feet, pulling Jacqui up with her.

"Your parents have 100 acres that they want to put horses on and you didn't tell us?" she asked, grinning from ear to ear.

Jacqui nodded slowly.

"So agistment is keeping horses?" Amelia questioned.

"Agistment is people paying to keep their horse on someone else's property," Hannah corrected her.

"Brilliant! Just brilliant," Geordie responded thoughtfully, sitting back down.

Jacqui sat down slowly, confused.

"What is?"

"Well... I've been thinking that even if I convince my parents to buy me a horse that I didn't have anywhere to keep her. And here you have the perfect solution – a property next door to where we ride! It's so close!"

"Geordie, aren't you forgetting something?" Hannah cut in.

The young red head looked to her brunette friend in surprise.

"What?"

"The cost?"

"Oh... yeah. Jacqui, how much is your mum going to charge for agistment at your property?"

"Umm... I don't know. I think we were focusing on getting the property right before working out other details... I'll ask her tonight," she promised.

Geordie grinned.

"Ok! Umm... do you think we could come and see your place?"

"Genesis?" Jacqui asked, surprised.

"Is that what the property's called?" Amelia asked.

Jacqui nodded.

"Then yes," Geordie responded with a grin, "can we come see Genesis? Maybe this weekend!"

Jacqui smiled.

"I'd love that but I'll have to ask my parents."

"For all of us?" Hannah asked, incredulous.

"I don't see why not. Maybe you can give ideas about what we should do to make the property appealing for agistment," she threw in, causing Geordie to grin again.

"Excellent! I think we should all go home and ask if it's ok that we spend Saturday or Sunday at Jacqui's place."

Jacqui faltered, unsure.

"Umm… perhaps Saturday? My family and I… we go to church on a Sunday morning," she explained, unsure.

"Saturday it is," Geordie responded simply, causing Jacqui to smile.

She was getting excited at the idea of her friends coming to visit. *And maybe they can help us with the property!* All too soon the bell went and the girls made their way off the oval, back to their classroom.

The following Saturday started cold and overcast. Jacqui was anxious about the girls coming to visit and not being able to see the property if it rained. Tony and Kate had thought it a wonderful idea for Jacqui to have some friends over on the weekend and said as much.

Ross had announced that he would be outside with Jack for the day if the house was going to be full of girls. Jacqui had smiled but understood. As the morning progressed however, she wondered if her brother would instead have to close himself away in his room.

Rain started lightly and built up in intensity as the morning passed. Jacqui wouldn't have been surprised if the girls had cancelled on her, but they all turned up after lunch, Geordie and Hannah together shortly followed by Amelia and then Caitlin.

Jacqui showed them around the house and then answered questions about the property as best she could. In their excitement, the girls agreed to put on their rain jackets and gumboots, and brave the weather.

Jacqui was relieved. She showed them the main area round the house and pointed out the further away paddocks, including the one that was next door to the East Riding School. Geordie was excited over seeing this.

Amelia and Caitlin were impressed, asking questions as they kept walking to stay warm. Only Hannah seemed bothered by the cold and wet.

The girls didn't brave the weather long, just long enough to see the individual paddocks and the area where Jacqui's mum thought they could put in some stables and an arena. Hannah stated at a glance that it looked like they would need to put in some shelters or more trees to help the horses hide from the cold and rain.

Jacqui agreed, telling of her plan to plant some trees with her mum.

Kate met the girls as they came in the door, announcing hot chocolate and biscuits were waiting for them at the kitchen table. They didn't need inviting twice.

Jacqui smiled as she warmed her hands around her mug. It was cold out!

"Mrs. King, how much are you planning to charge for agistment?" Geordie asked, Jacqui realising she'd forgotten on more than one occasion to ask for her friend.

Kate smiled.

"It seems to me that the going rate around here varies a lot. I think it would be better to charge a lump sum per calendar month, rather than weekly. This'll make it cheaper for people in the long run as they'll only have to pay for 12 months, instead of 13 lots of four weeks. I was thinking fifty dollars a month."

Geordie grinned.

"That would be affordable if I had a job!" she replied, earning a laugh from Jacqui's mum.

"It's not a lot, but at the moment we can only offer grass, water and fences. We may be able to charge more if we create some private paddocks and get an arena in but there are some things we need to fix up before we start advertising our services."

Kate told the girls to help themselves to more drink if they needed and headed into the spare bedroom that she'd developed into an office.

Geordie obliged, taking a biscuit from the plate in front of her. Ross entered the kitchen long enough to get a hot chocolate and some biscuits. Then he retreated back to his room.

Jacqui felt sorry for him that he couldn't enjoy being outside.

"Who was that?" Amelia asked Jacqui, eyes wide.

"My brother Ross. He goes to the high school around the corner from our school," she replied simply, sipping from her drink.

Caitlin laughed, causing Jacqui to look at her in surprise.

"I think Amelia's in love," she stated with a knowing smile.

Amelia blushed.

"I am not!"

Jacqui smiled, changing the topic to avoid embarrassing her further. The girls played a couple of board games as the rain grew heavier outside. As the afternoon grew late they announced that they should be going home.

Jacqui agreed, disappointed that she hadn't been able to show them more of the property. Hannah left first, followed by Amelia and Caitlin.

Geordie had asked if it was ok that she stayed a bit longer. Her brother Johnny was going to pick her up after he'd finished work as it was close by. Jacqui agreed, happy to spend some more time with the most friendly of the four.

"I don't think Hannah likes me very much," she confided in Geordie once the others had gone.

"Yeah... she's jealous. Don't worry, she'll get over it and then you'll find she's really nice. I promise."

Jacqui frowned.

"What's she jealous of?"

"You, duh! Hannah and I have always been crazy about horses. I love learning about them and how to be a better rider. Hannah's more competitive and loves to win things. Recently she's been winning most little tests we've been set by our horse riding instructor Emmy and I think it's made her a bit proud. And now, well we've met you and although you don't know how to ride yet, you have this really cool property and it looks like once your parents get you a horse, you'll be able to ride all day, every day!" she explained, causing Jacqui to laugh.

"I'll still have school," she reasoned.

Geordie rolled her eyes.

"Details, details," she replied, glancing around the house.

"So can I see your room?" she asked suddenly.

Jacqui shrugged.

"Ok, sure. It's nothing special. Oh, but I can show you this horse book mum gave me! I'm learning lots from it."

She led the way down the hallway, Geordie following behind. As they entered Geordie went straight to the window that Jacqui had gazed out of on first arriving to Genesis.

"I'm sure the view is great when it's not windy and raining!" she said appreciatively.

Jacqui agreed that it was.

"I was so excited when we first moved here and I could see the back two paddocks right from sitting on my bed," she replied with a grin.

Geordie turned around and sat on the bed, looking back through the window. She placed her hands behind her head and lay back with a sigh.

"This is the life! Hey! What are you doing with a horse riding helmet?" she asked suddenly, seeing Jacqui's helmet hanging on the back of the bedroom door.

"Oh... that. Umm... I guess I didn't tell you guys something," Jacqui started, causing Geordie to sit up on the bed.

"So?" she prompted, her legs crossed in front of her.

"Well when I said no to your birthday party because I couldn't ride, that was true. But... there's an older girl on the other side of our property who has a horse. I was out walking sometime and met her and she offered to teach me to horse ride."

"That's so cool!" Geordie enthused, "so when will you start?"

Jacqui grinned.

"Actually, I had my first ride on the day of your birthday party. Kara – that's the girl – met my parents and then she gave me a riding lesson. Banjo – that's her horse – is so quiet! Kara led me around, teaching me about steering as well as starting and stopping. Once I was happy with that, she let me have a little trot. She was kind enough to let me ride again on the Sunday after church. I think I've almost got the rising trot now," Jacqui stated proudly.

Geordie grinned.

"I think we should keep this a secret from the others for now. But how cool will it be when we're all able to ride together on this property?"

Jacqui nodded, smiling widely. She couldn't think of anything more appealing at that moment.

The girls chattered late into the afternoon, Geordie teaching Jacqui some more basics about horses before talking about what could be done with the property. They started a list of things that they would want on their dream property and took it to Kate before Geordie went home.

Jacqui's mum accepted it with delight, an idea touching her. She decided to discuss it with her husband before mentioning it to her daughter and friend.

Jacqui went to sleep that night content. She'd missed out on a lesson with Kara because of the rain, but thought she probably would have anyway with her friends visiting for the afternoon. As she lay in bed ready for sleep, she thanked her God for the new friends that she'd made and how exciting the future seemed at that time.

Seven

Over the months that followed, Jacqui spent a lot of time planning the property with her mother and talking about it at school with her friends. The girls had come over to Genesis as a group again and Jacqui was relieved to find that Hannah was being nicer to her.

Geordie had come over a few times by herself, talking with Jacqui about what they'd learn in their riding lesson. Some of the information Jacqui found she'd been able to use in her lessons with Kara.

Much to her delight, she'd been able to continue these on a weekly basis, both on Saturday and Sunday afternoons. After a month of practicing the rising and sitting trot, Kara had insisted that Jacqui not be on the lead anymore, taking Banjo by herself.

"Besides, I'm not fit enough to keep running beside you the number of times you want to trot!" she'd stated jokingly, causing Jacqui to smile.

The young girl had been unsure at first, but found that Banjo was willing to listen to her. He was very obedient and responded to the slightest aid that Jacqui used to communicate with. She loved that she only had to squeeze a little with her legs and he increased his speed. He was also quick to respond to her pressure on the reins meaning stop.

Kara had surprised her by mentioning that she could stop Banjo by stopping her 'seat'. Jacqui had asked and found out that Kara meant as she stopped the middle of her body moving, it communicated with Banjo that he should stop moving. Jacqui had decided then that when she got her pony, she'd love to be able to do the same thing.

Another four weeks passed and Jacqui was proficiently working with Banjo, walking and trotting in whichever direction she wanted. Kara taught her about rising diagonals of the trot, explaining when she should rise out of the saddle and when she should sit.

Jacqui asked why it mattered when she rose and sat and Kara patiently explained about it being easier for the horse's balance if they were working on a circle or going around a corner. She pointed out that it didn't matter so much when they were going in a straight line.

Jacqui was also taught the sitting trot. She found this very bouncy and uncomfortable after learning to rise to the trot. She said so to Kara.

Kara laughed and said that once Jacqui learnt it well, Kara would teach her how to do something really cool on a horse. Jacqui took her at her word, working hard to learn the sitting and rising trot well.

After eight weeks of riding, Kara put Jacqui back onto a lead and explained that she felt Jacqui had learnt the sitting trot well enough to learn something new.

"Is that why I need to be on a lead again?" Jacqui asked, thinking that she loved being able to guide Banjo around as she pleased.

"Yup! Today we're going to canter!" Kara replied enthusiastically.

Jacqui felt her body tense.

"But I don't know how to canter," she replied quietly.

Kara smiled encouragingly.

"Jacqui, you didn't know how to walk, steer, stop or trot either and you've learnt all of those really well! That's why I wanted you to learn the sitting trot. It's important to do before we ask our horse to canter so that we're already sitting as we will be at the canter. It's a lot smoother than the sitting trot, I promise!"

Jacqui smiled, still nervous.

"Ok... but if the canter's faster than the trot, how are you going to keep up with us?"

Kara smiled and pointed to the lead in her hand.

"Have you noticed how this is a bit different to the lead rope we normally use?"

Jacqui looked down at the thin, long black lead and nodded.

"This is called a lunging rope. I'm going to stand in the middle, holding one end of it and you're going to get Banjo to walk a large circle around me with the other end attached to his bridle like it already is. Once you're comfortable, you're going to ask him to trot, do some rising trot and then when you're happy you can go into a sitting trot."

Jacqui nodded, digesting the information.

"Now this bit's important. I've been teaching you about aids that we use to communicate with the horse. Well the way that Banjo knows to canter is that I put my inside leg against his girth and my outside leg a bit behind it and I squeeze. Have I taught you about inside and outside legs?" Kara asked, clarifying.

Jacqui nodded, thinking.

"If we're going in a circle around to the right, then my inside leg is my right leg because it'll be closest to you in the middle?"

Kara nodded, smiling.

"Great Jacqui! Do you have any questions?"

"What do I do once we're cantering?"

"Sit up nice and tall and just stay sitting in the saddle and looking towards where you want to go. You may want to lean back a little bit as this helps you to sit taller... and once you're ready to stop, just apply some pressure to Banjo's reins. Then you can go back to the rising trot."

Jacqui nodded, pushing Banjo into a walk as Kara encouraged her to. She easily increased the pace to a trot and rose up down, up down until Kara reminded her that she would need to be sitting before the canter.

Once she was ready, Jacqui sat deeply into the saddle, bouncing a little bit. After a few strides of the trot she put her legs where Kara had said and squeezed.

Banjo continued trotting.

Jacqui tried again, squeezing harder this time before kicking a little. The bay gelding got the message and changed the sequence of his legs, now doing a 3 beat canter.

"Great job!" Kara called out, watching Jacqui grin as she sat up tall, only bouncing a little bit with the larger stride of the canter.

Jacqui laughed, loving the feeling of cantering along on Banjo.

"This is great!" she called out breathlessly.

After a lap Kara suggested she come back to a trot. Jacqui applied pressure to the reins, finding herself bouncing a lot as Banjo slowed down.

"Hold on, Jacqui!" Kara called out, watching the young girl lose her balance.

Jacqui found herself fall forward on Banjo's neck as he slowed down to a walk. She pulled on the reins to ask Banjo to stop before lying with her arms around his neck.

"Are you ok?" Kara asked, heading toward the pair.

Jacqui sat up slowly and nodded.

"So! Can we try a canter in the other direction?"

Kara laughed, relieved.

"Sure! But maybe we can just walk a bit first so that you can get some strength back! It can be difficult to keep your balance when you come back from the canter."

Jacqui nodded. The girls chattered away as Jacqui walked to catch her breath.

"I just realised something… are you getting to ride Banjo often enough Kara?"

Kara nodded and smiled.

"I ride him 2 to 3 times during the week after school and sometimes if I feel we haven't done a lot over the weekend, I'll do something with him afterward. He's a very fit boy at the moment from two girls loving him!"

Jacqui smiled.

"But I also really enjoy helping you learn to ride, Jacqui... and watching as things fall into place. It's making me think that maybe I could pursue instructing horse riding as a job when I'm a bit older and I've got more riding experienced."

"I think you're a great instructor!" Jacqui remarked, causing Kara to smile again.

"Thanks! Now will we try a canter on the left lead this time?"

Jacqui nodded and the girls finished off their lesson on this note. Kara told Jacqui that because she'd managed to canter; their next lesson would be focused on going over some small jumps. Jacqui excitedly told her she looked forward to it.

Jacqui excitedly gave Geordie a run down of her lesson from the weekend where she'd gotten to canter. She also mentioned Kara suggesting they try jumping the next lesson. Geordie was thrilled to hear of her friend's progress.

"So, I was wondering, what are horse jumps made out of?" Jacqui asked, causing Geordie to smile.

"What are you two talking about?" Hannah asked, joining them at the classroom tables.

Jacqui smiled.

"I was curious about what horse jumps are made out of. I think the more I can learn, the better," she responded, seeing Geordie's relieved smile.

They still hadn't told the other girls about Jacqui's riding lessons.

"They can be made out of lots of things!" Hannah responded with a smile as she sat down beside Geordie.

"Like what?"

"Well most of the ones at the East Riding School are big barrels that they call 44 gallon drums; or some sort of steel wings that have little hooks or cups that they rest these long round poles on. They also have big plastic drums that they use to put the poles on. I think as long as they have two solid things at each end, they can then put a pole across them for the horses to jump."

Geordie nodded enthusiastically.

"I've seen at other places people using tyres, piling them up on top of each other, old wooden chairs that they put far apart and face back to back, with the bit you jump resting from one chair to the other... I think anything that is easy for the horse to see and isn't spiky is pretty good!"

Jacqui grinned.

"So I should get mum to start collecting our old car tyres anytime they get them changed on the car," she joked.

Hannah nodded.

"You should! I've even seen a round yard made up of tyres joined together in a circle."

"A round yard?" Jacqui queried, not sure what that was.

"Yeah, it's this yard that is circular in shape that you can use to exercise a horse... like lunging, have you heard of lunging?" Geordie asked.

Jacqui nodded, thinking of her first canter lesson with Kara.

"So… do you lunge a horse with a person on?"

"Sometimes. But Emmy's told us that they also do it with a horse to see how it's moving, to teach it to trot and canter on voice command and to get rid of extra energy before they ride. It could be a really cool thing for your parents to have at Genesis."

Jacqui grinned, picturing all the things they could do with tyres.

"I think I'll definitely have to tell mum about collecting tyres!" she said, saying hello to Caitlin and Amelia as they raced into class in time for the 9 o'clock bell.

Quickly Mr O'Laughlin called the class to attention with the roll. Jacqui smiled as she realised that they would read the last two chapters of their novel for the term before completing some questions and answers. It would be an easy morning as far as she was concerned.

She reminded herself that she should focus, but found herself writing a list of things they could do with tyres in her school diary. She couldn't wait to get home and talk with her mum!

Eight

Kate sighed with content as she tended the vegetable garden with Tony, Ross and Jacqui. It was a rare Saturday morning that her two children didn't have any outstanding assignments or homework and she'd taken advantage of this to spend some time with her children and husband.

Young Jack their kelpie ran from each pile of dirt that was being turned over, sniffing in case there was anything of interest to him. Tony had spent a couple of weekends erecting boxes to put around the mounds that Kate had built up of soil and then put vegetables into.

They had four boxes in total out the back of their house. So far only two were being used, but Kate envisaged all four full of home grown vegetables in the future.

They were working in the third box that weekend, planting a lot of seeds that had been waiting for the warmer spring months. Jacqui was eager to plant every seed they had in the packets that Kate had purchased from a nearby garden store.

Kate smiled.

"Do you remember that verse in the bible about planting a crop and yielding many times more than you plant?" she asked her daughter.

Ross grinned and nudged Jacqui in the side with an elbow.

"Look out, here comes a bible lesson," he said cheekily, ducking as Tony threw some dirt at him.

Jacqui nodded.

"A bible lesson that is always timely," Tony retaliated with a smile of his own.

"Well the same works for us with these seeds, Jacqui. For each seed that we plant, if we water it and it gets sun, it should be able to make use of the nutrients in the soil to help it grow. Eventually each plant produce fruit that has as many seeds in them as this packet that we're starting with. If we're smart, we'll collect some of those seeds but we can keep some from this packet to plant at another time just in case something goes wrong with these plants. Does that make sense?"

Jacqui nodded, thinking it over.

"So how many seeds will we get from the ones that we plant?"

"I'm not sure. That depends on how well the seed grows and how much we look after it. Another reason for us to not plant all of the seeds now is that we can plant a few more in a month's time. That'll mean that when the first plants stop producing food, the second ones will probably have started. We won't need to do much fresh food shopping then!" Kate stated with glee, causing her husband to laugh.

"What?" she asked Tony with a smile, "the more we can save by eating from our garden, the more we can invest into the property. Did I tell you about Jacqui's idea for a round yard?"

Tony rolled his eyes, causing Ross to laugh and throw some dirt at his father.

"Here's a timely horse finance lesson for you, dad," he stated helpfully.

Tony laughed.

"Touché!"

"Don't worry, the round yard and jumps won't cost us much! We just need to work out where to get the tyres from," Jacqui stated, carefully placing dirt over the been seeds she'd put in a row under her mum's guidance.

"Jumps as well!" Tony stated in surprise.

"Of course, dad! The more things we are able to provide on this property, the more people will want to keep their horses here because they can also ride them and have fun," Jacqui stated sincerely, causing her brother and father to smile in amusement.

Jack raced off around the front of the house, barking suddenly. Tony looked up in surprise. A car horn tooted, causing Kate to smile.

"Speaking of building things and saving money!" she said cryptically, standing to her feet and wiping her hands across her jeans.

"Jacqui, did you want to come and say hi to Hannah?" she asked, causing her daughter to look up in surprise.

"Hannah's here?"

"I think she would be! Your friend rang up a couple of nights ago to ask if we could make use of some tyres that her father was going to take to the tip. Did you know her dad's a mechanic and often fits tyres for people?"

Jacqui shook her head.

"I told her over the phone that we'd be delighted to take any tyres that they could give us. I think she'd been pondering your want of tyres for jumps and a round yard," Kate said knowingly, causing Jacqui to smile.

She raced after her mum and dad, eager to see what Hannah had brought with her father.

Hannah waited shyly with her father, standing outside the car. She was looking around at the property. She smiled in relief when she spied Jacqui.

"Hi! You guys have been busy!"

Jacqui smiled proudly.

"Yeah! Dad and Ross have been levelling out this area for an arena and they cleaned out that old shed. Dad thinks he should be able to fit four lots of posts and rails in the shed, which will mean that five horses can be tied up in there, under cover!" she explained excitedly.

Hannah's eyes lit up.

"Really? That's so cool! When do you think that'll happen?"

Jacqui shrugged and laughed.

"It may get put on hold until some jumps and a round yard are made," she stated cheekily, causing Hannah to laugh.

"I was thinking about you asking about what jumps could be made out of... so that afternoon I went home and asked dad if he had any old tyres at work. He was suspicious at first but when I explained why, he suggested I give your mum a call to check if she actually wanted them."

"I'm so glad you did!" Jacqui stated honestly.

The girls worked together with their parents to carry tyres from the trailer that Hannah's dad had brought. It was decided that 50 would be a starting point for the round yard and the few left over would be piled together nearby for some jumps.

Jacqui excitedly took in the large piles of tyres, already imagining a round yard and a heap of jumps that she, Hannah and Geordie could jump whilst racing around on their own ponies. *I can't wait for that to happen!*

Hannah had wanted to stay longer but her dad needed to get going. He promised Kate that he would contact her the next time he had a build up of tyres at the workshop. Mrs. King thanked him gratefully.

Jacqui waved goodbye to the pair as they headed back down the drive. She turned to her parents with a huge grin.

"How cool is that!"

"Isn't it amazing how when you speak to others about something that excites you, God gets them excited enough to help out?" Kate asked with a grin, Tony's arm around her shoulders.

Jacqui smiled as she thought about what Kate had said.

"It sure is! I'm so glad we moved here," she added, causing her parents to smile.

Ross let out a low whistle as he came around the corner of the house.

"That's a lot of tyres! What on earth are you going to do with them?"

"We," Tony corrected with a grin, "are going to make a round yard, my dear boy. I think your mother and sister will perhaps make use of Jacqui's friends and create some jumps."

Tony turned his gaze to his wife.

"I think that we should start advertising agistment at Genesis."

Jacqui clapped her hands in glee.

"Yes!"

"Are you sure? I thought we should have the place in better condition. It'll be more ready for horses when we have shelters up, the round yard done, the tie up area…"

"It's ready now! The fences are in working order, each paddock has sufficient gates and water and there are trees in patches that will provide protection. The rest we can add to improve the property as time permits. Besides, it may take awhile to generate interest and even customers."

Kate nodded, thinking over what Tony had said.

"I think you're right," she stated with a smile, reaching up to kiss him.

"Of course I am!" Tony replied modestly, causing her to laugh.

Jacqui was busy explaining to her brother about how big the round yard needed to be so that horses could be exercised in it. Ross tried to take in all the information as Jacqui talked a mile a minute. In the ended he decided it was easier to just nod and ask his father later.

"I have to tell you guys something," Hannah blurted out suddenly.

The girls had just sat down to lunch. Four pairs of eyes looked at Hannah curiously.

"I have an aunt who lives a few hours away that breeds Australian Riding and Welsh Mountain ponies. Mum and dad have told me that for my birthday next year, they're happy to buy me a pony from her," she gushed out, her face flushed in pleasure.

Geordie squealed, leaping up to hug her friend.

"I can't believe you didn't tell me on the phone last night! And what about our recess break?!" she demanded, still hugging her friend tightly.

"I couldn't get a word in at recess!" Hannah bit back, looking at Amelia with a grin.

Amelia blushed. She'd been asked out by one of the other year five boys and hadn't stopped talking about it all morning.

Jacqui looked at Hannah in awe. *She's getting a pony!* She smiled in excitement for her friend.

"So when's your birthday?"

"February 17. And do you know the best bit? Mum and dad want to be sure that I'm comfortable with the horse that they buy, so they've spoken with my aunt Jan and she's invited me to stay over the summer holidays to try out a pony! I'll stay with her for two weeks, then mum and dad will come pick me and my pony up and I'll trial him or her for another month or so before my parents agree to buy it."

"That is so cool!" Caitlin said, the others nodding in agreement.

"And there's more," Hannah continued with a huge smile.

"More?" Jacqui asked, curious.

"I told my aunt about how horse mad we are," Hannah stated matter of fact, "and she told me that you're all welcome to come with me to stay over the holidays and ride her ponies!"

Geordie squealed again, hugging her best friend. Hannah laughed at Geordie's excitement.

"Does that mean you'll come?"

"Of course!" Geordie replied, looking to Jacqui for her response.

"If my parents say yes, then I'm in!" she replied, Caitlin and Amelia nodding in agreement.

The girls spent the rest of their lunch time discussing their dream horses. Jacqui found herself day dreaming through their afternoon math class. In her mind she was cantering along happily on her little grey pony, jumping anything that happened to be in their path in the back paddock at Genesis. *What a dream!*

Nine

Jacqui stood up as the kids were dismissed, gesturing for Geordie to follow her. It was Sunday morning and they were at church.

Geordie had asked if she could come and help out at the property over the weekend. Jacqui had mentioned that her mum was going to make some jumps whilst Tony and Ross started the round yard.

Hannah had jumped at the idea of helping too and Jacqui had invited the pair over. Kate had suggested that her daughter might like to have a sleep over so that the girls could continue their fun on the Sunday.

Hannah hadn't liked the idea of spending a morning at church so had agreed to come back on Sunday afternoon after lunch. Geordie had decided she'd like to try out church however, and so she'd slept over and went along with the Kings to their local church.

Whilst the adults were listening to a sermon, the children were invited to attend kids' church, where they were often taught a bible story and given some puzzles to work out or games to play.

The theme for the term was personal worth. This Sunday's lesson was focused on being a person with integrity.

"It's great for us to be accountable for our actions and words," their leader informed them, looking around at the group of 12 or so children with a smile.

"One of the ways we can do this is by making use of our friends. So tell me, how many of you have good friends?" they were asked.

Every person put up their hand to indicate that they did. Jacqui smiled as she thought of Geordie in particular, but also of Hannah, Amelia and Caitlin. She sure had some good friends!

"Often our friends are people that we like, have things in common with and sometimes we even believe the same things. For example, I believe that chocolate is the best food you can possibly get," their kid's church leader joked.

Jacqui laughed along with Geordie.

"But if I have a friend that doesn't like chocolate, that's ok! If however, I have a friend that believes it's ok to lie and steal, then I may decide that that person and I are better to not be friends. I have a choice about who my friends are. I also have a choice about what I do or don't do. Sometimes I can use friends to encourage me to be a good person. Who here isn't so keen on homework?"

A few hands shot up around the room, Geordie's included. Jacqui smiled at this. She enjoyed learning and believed that that was why they were given homework.

"And who knows that if we don't do our homework, there are consequences… and that these consequences usually aren't good?"

All of the hands in the room went up.

"That's right! So we have a choice to either do our homework, or not do it and deal with the bad consequences. A great thing about having friends is that they may be able to help us with our homework, or even remind us when something is due if we're likely to forget! Friends can help to remind us about the way we want to act. This is called being accountable."

Jacqui thought that maybe she should offer to help Geordie with her English homework. Maybe Hannah would like to help too. It seemed to Jacqui that Geordie's strong point was math, while Hannah and Jacqui both loved English. Amelia and Caitlin seemed more interested in sports.

Jacqui decided she would discuss this with Geordie when she got a chance. She'd gotten into a habit of doing her homework as soon as she got home because of the routine that her parents encouraged her and Ross to follow.

Jacqui didn't know if this was the same for Geordie, but she did know that her friend would at times use lunch time to quickly finish a task that had been set the week before. Jacqui decided then that if Geordie wanted, she could help to keep her accountable for her school work.

When the lesson was finished for the morning, the group of children were given a crossword to work out, based on the key words they'd discussed. Jacqui finished it easily, discussing her answers with Geordie.

Because of her love of chocolate, their leader gave them each a chocolate frog before sending them on their way, reminding them to think about the sort of person they'd like to be and who could help keep them accountable.

That afternoon Geordie, Hannah and Jacqui had fun painting tyres bright colours with different patterns. Tony had cut some of the tyres in half, planning to put two long pieces of wood between these as a jump.

Other tyres were left whole to be piled on top of each other horizontally. This way the jump could be increased or decreased in size as the riders wanted them to be at the time.

Kate had found some paint on sale and had purchased some prior to the weekend, thinking the girls would enjoy painting the jumps. She wasn't wrong.

"So have you decided what type of pony you want?" Jacqui asked, having had a picture of her ideal horse in her mind for a long time.

Hannah smiled.

"I'd love to have a chestnut with some white socks and a blaze. I'm not sure if I'd prefer a mare or a gelding, though."

Jacqui nodded, aware that a mare was a female and a gelding was a castrated male. It wasn't safe for younger inexperienced riders to be around a stallion. They could be too strong and unpredictable.

"I read somewhere that geldings can be more quiet... something about them not being so moody or changeable," Jacqui stated, thinking about the recent horse book she'd borrowed from the school library.

"Well I want a mare!" Geordie stated with conviction. "If I could buy Sheila from the East Riding School, I'd have her!"

"Have you asked?" Jacqui asked, curious.

"Yeah. They suggested that I might like to purchase a younger horse – Sheila's 20 – and that she was too valuable as a riding pony for many people for them to consider selling her," Geordie sighed.

"Well maybe you can find one like her," Jacqui suggested, painting some blue dots onto the light purple tyre she was working on.

Hannah nodded.

"Have you asked your parents yet about whether you could get a horse from my Aunt's place?"

Geordie nodded.

"They still want to know where we'll keep her and how much it's going to cost. I think if I could solve that problem… oh, and improve my school work, then I'd be set!"

"Have your parents said something about your schoolwork?" Jacqui asked; thinking about their lesson in kid's church.

"Yeah… mum doesn't think I'm responsible enough with school work. Dad has suggested if I take school more seriously, it might give them some confidence about me looking after a horse."

"So we need to improve your grades and find you some cheap agistment," Jacqui stated thoughtfully, Geordie and Hannah nodding in agreement.

"How's the painting going?" Kate asked, bringing some drinks and cut up fruit for the girls.

"Great!" Geordie responded enthusiastically, causing Kate to smile.

"Mrs. King, have you decided on a price for agistment yet?"

"We sure have, Geordie. We decided on fifty dollars a month. Actually, I wanted to talk with you girls about that. Jacqui told me that Hannah will soon be getting a pony."

The girls nodded.

"Well I don't know if you've thought about where you'll keep your pony, Hannah, but I've got a proposition for you girls. If you're happy to help out at Genesis for a couple of hours, three times a week, then Tony and I would be delighted to offer you free agistment in return."

Geordie looked at Jacqui's mum, her mouth open in surprise. Hannah nodded enthusiastically, grinning.

"I'd love that! I'd want to see my pony as often as possible anyway, so if I was down here to visit him or her, then it'd be easy to help out! What would I have to do?"

"I think it would depend on the time of year and how things are going around the property. I can think of a few things such as painting jumps, helping pick up paddocks or yards, keeping the tie up area clean, cleaning out grooming brushes, that kind of thing. Discuss it with your parents and let me know what you think," Kate finished with a smile, walking back to the house.

Geordie grinned at Jacqui, making her feel uncomfortable.

"What?" she asked defensively.

"I think I love your parents!" she replied enthusiastically, causing Jacqui to burst out laughing.

"And I think we've solved your problems!" she replied, causing Geordie to frown in confusion.

"What problems?"

"The agistment and school problem we were just talking about! Mum's solved the money problem for you and I've been thinking about our lesson at Church this morning. I really like getting school work done early so that I don't have to worry about it later in the week. Plus, mum and dad won't let me do other things I want to until my homework is done. What if we met together mid week to do homework together?"

Geordie screwed up her nose at the idea of studying. Hannah gave her a gentle shove.

"It's a great idea, Geordie. Say yes! Then maybe your parents will see you being responsible and they'll let you buy a pony from my Aunt!"

Geordie nodded in agreement.

"Ok, ok! It's a good thing I've got friends like you to keep me on track," she joked, causing them to laugh and get back to their painting.

Geordie was eager for her mum to come pick her up that afternoon. Now that she had a plan ready to be put into action, she wanted to make sure her parents would agree to buying her a pony!

Her mother greeted her as she raced down the drive toward the car.

"I thought I'd have to drag you away from your friends and here you are running towards the car!" she stated in wonder, smiling at her daughter.

"Hi mum! I had the best time! It looks like Jacqui's parents will have their property open for agistment soon and guess what Jacqui's mum offered Hannah and I? If we're willing to help out around the property a few times a week, then they're willing to give us free agistment!"

Mrs. Smith smiled, biting back a chuckle at her daughter's extreme enthusiasm.

"That sounds wonderful... but what about your school work?"

"I was talking with Jacqui and Hannah about that today. They were talking about something at church this morning that made Jacqui think of a solution to that problem! She suggested that she could meet up with me each week to get on top of school work. Starting from next week we're going to get together each Wednesday afternoon and spend however much time is needed for me to finish my homework."

"That sounds very wise. So what did they talk about at the church?" Geordie's mother asked as she drove her daughter home.

"Umm... accounting!" she replied after some thought.

"You mean... something to do with money?"

"No, doing things that you should and having friends help you to behave."

Geordie's mother laughed.

"Accountability?" she queried.

Geordie grinned.

"That's it! It seemed a good idea to me, to have a friend that can work with you to be a good person and I really liked their music. If Jacqui's parents say it's ok, do you think I could go again, mum?"

Mrs. Smith shrugged.

"I don't see why not, darling. Check with Jacqui and I'm sure she can ask them for you."

"And can I get a horse when I go with Hannah to her Aunt's place?" she asked hopefully.

"I won't say no to that request, but I won't say yes either. Let's see how your study with Jacqui goes and I want you to call up the Kings when we get home and say that you'd like to start helping out at their property next week. If you can demonstrate to me that you're taking this seriously... then we can talk ponies at the end of the year," Mrs. Smith told her daughter, earning an excited squeal in return.

Ten

Geordie followed her mum's instructions and rang the Kings that night about helping out at the property. Kate had been surprised but more than pleased.

Jacqui had laughed when she'd talked with Geordie after her mum had finished. She was excited to see that her friend was acting out things that would help her get a horse.

The fact that Hannah was getting a horse the following year and that Geordie's parents would consider it if she improved her attitude to school and outside responsibilities made the young blonde haired girl excited. Because her friends were closer to getting a horse, it felt like she was too!

Jacqui's mum had created flyers to hang up around town and given some to Jacqui to hand out to friends at school that she wanted to. Tony had created a simple website and he and Ross were working hard on two signs that they would put at the end of their driveway and at the end of their property on Rivers Road.

The sign simply stated Genesis – Agistment Available and their contact details. It seemed that things were moving forward at a rapid pace for the whole family.

Kate was thankful for weekends where she could invest her energy into something that her heart desired. She'd managed to pick up a part time job that had grown from 15 hours a week to 30. The mother of 2 was grateful for the opportunity to earn extra income.

Leasing Genesis wasn't cheap and she and Tony were aware that once they had customers making use of the facilities, repairs would be a commonplace task. Of course it was anticipated that the customers would be paying for the agistment, but it was important to plan for a situation where cash flow wasn't as free and easy as they would like.

Jacqui got into a habit of doing a lot of her school work over lunchtime whilst her friends chattered around her. They didn't mind as long as she joined in the conversation.

This way the young girl could race home, change and get working on the property with her mum. This was especially important on Mondays, Wednesdays and Fridays when Geordie and Hannah joined her.

As soon as Hannah had heard that Geordie was already helping out at Genesis in anticipation of getting a pony, she'd volunteered too. The girls caught the bus back to Jacqui's place together and were later picked up by their parents.

On a Wednesday afternoon the three stayed later together at school, making use of the library and school computers. They talked a lot about horses but Jacqui kept them on track with getting their study done, too. She reasoned with Geordie when motivation was low, that they wouldn't get to go work on the property until all three had finished their homework. This seemed to do the trick.

That Wednesday afternoon the girls came home to find Jacqui's mother having already piled up their utility vehicle with a large amount of trees. Jacqui looked at them in surprise.

"There was a sale on and I've been reading that trees should be planted as soon as the weather is good and you know where to put them! The sooner we put them in, the bigger they'll get over time for the horses and provide shade and wind protection," she informed the girls, causing them to smile.

"I'll quickly get changed!" Jacqui replied, racing to the house with her two friends in tow eager to do the same.

Dressed in more appropriate gear for working outside than their school uniforms, the girls squeezed into the cab with Kate. She drove first to the paddock located behind the house, stopping at a point where she'd already dug a few holes.

"I've been thinking that we need names for our paddocks," Kate suggested as she directed the girls to put some gloves on and help her drag the trees off the back of the ute.

"Names?" Hannah asked, unsure.

"Sure. When people are keeping their horses here, it'll be good to be able to tell them which paddock they can find their horse in. Over time as they get used to the property, I can direct them around by the names of each of the paddocks."

Geordie nodded enthusiastically.

"The East Riding School next door sort of do that, don't you remember Hannah? We get our riding school horses out of the pony paddock, there's a Galloway paddock and a mare paddock."

"But that changes, depending on where the ponies, Galloways and mares are!" Hannah replied, not thinking this to be the same thing.

"I guess so... but we always get our horses from the pony paddock and take them back to it," she argued, causing Jacqui to giggle.

"I think this one should be called the house paddock. Is that too simple?" she asked her mum.

Kate smiled.

"It's perfect. So if the one that sits behind the house is the house paddock, what about the one that sits behind that?"

"Hmmm... well it's at the back, so maybe back paddock, or rivers paddock because it's on rivers road?" Hannah suggested, getting into the swing of things.

Geordie nodded.

"Back paddock is easy to remember! What about the one to the left of the house?"

The girls were quiet with concentration, pausing from piling in dirt around the trees. Kate told them to get back to work, teasing. The three laughed but did so.

"What about the arena paddock? I know it's not set up yet, but technically that's where we plan on having it," Jacqui's mother suggested.

The three girls looked at each other and shrugged.

"Arena paddock it is!" Geordie announced.

"I think the small one up the front could be the driveway paddock," Hannah interjected.

"Well that just leaves us with the paddock that is near the freeway," Jacqui declared, pleased with their work in naming the paddocks so far.

"You mean the freeway paddock?" Geordie suggested with a grin.

Kate laughed.

"I love it! It's simple and people should be able to remember their names based on their locations. Well now we have two new signs, a website, some new trees in and names for our paddocks... now all we need are the customers," she joked, causing the girls to smile.

"I just realised I should be praying for them!" Jacqui stated in alarm, "Do you think that's why we don't have any yet?"

Kate smiled fondly at her daughter.

"I don't think so, honey. Your prayers would be wonderful, but things will happen in God's timing. We can get impatient at times and want everything now... sort of like you three all wanting a pony already," Kate mentioned, causing the three girls to nod in agreement.

"It'll happen! Until then, we just need to enjoy now and keep working towards what we want. And for Genesis, that means planting more trees! Come on, hop back in the cab and we'll plant some more down this fence line before heading on to the back paddock," she suggested.

The girls followed her instruction, finishing patting dirt around their trees before hopping back into the car.

They spent the next hour or so planting the trees that Kate had put onto the back of the ute.

Eleven

Kate yawned and stretched her arms, thinking it was well and truly time for her to go to bed. She put her pen down from an invoice she'd been creating for Genesis. Looking from the kitchen into the lounge room she smiled. Tony was dozing on the couch, the television running quietly in the background with no one watching it.

She got up from her seat and walked into the room to turn it off. Tony roused from his slumber, taking a moment to orient himself.

Kate smiled and walked over to her husband, kissing him on the forehead.

"Bed time?" she suggested quietly.

Tony nodded and made his way to his feet, looking around the room. He glanced up at the clock that hung in the lounge room.

"It's only half past eight! Where are the kids?"

"In bed already, would you believe it?" Kate asked with a smile.

As the pair got ready for bed, Kate told her husband of her afternoon planting with Jacqui and the girls. She mentioned that the physical labour might be what had tired their daughter out. Tony nodded in agreement.

"It's wonderful to see she's made such good friends and that they're helping each other be responsible. I'm so proud of Jacqui. So what's Ross' excuse for being in bed at a decent hour?" Tony asked with a grin.

Kate laughed.

"He's got a test tomorrow and said that he wanted to get up early to go over the test points. You know how he's more alert in the mornings than later at night."

Tony nodded again and reached out for his wife, pulling her into his embrace.

"I already knew that we had great kids and that we'll still have challenges, but it seems that this transfer has been a good thing for our family."

Kate nodded, accepting a kiss from him.

"I think you're right! Now if we could just turn Genesis into a viable business option, then I could spend more time at home with the kids instead of in a job that helps to pay the bills," she commented hopefully.

Tony smiled.

"I guess we should be adding that to the prayer list. It's either that, or my wife has an attitude change and falls in love with her current job," he joked, ducking as Kate tried to hit him with a pillow.

The pair settled into bed, thanking God for the day and for His protection of their kids. They offered up requests for their children, their property and working lives before collapsing into a deep sleep.

Jacqui sighed, pulling the front door shut behind her before dumping her bag in her room and changing into shorts and a t-shirt. It was hot!

She got herself a cool drink out of the fridge before going in search of her mother. Kate was out the back picking some tomatoes from their overflowing veggie garden. Jacqui joined her, putting the cherry tomatoes into a bowl her mum had brought outside.

"Long day?" Kate asked knowingly, thinking the end of the school term couldn't come fast enough for her youngest child.

"Yeah... I guess it's good that they use the last week of school to introduce us to what the following year's going to be like... but today they gave us our English books that we need to read for next year and do you know that I should have the first one read before I start school? And then they took us through some math which seems a bit hard to me... I think next year is going to be difficult."

Kate squeezed her daughter's shoulder encouragingly.

"Just take each day as it comes, honey. It seems to me that you've forgotten that you love to read! I'm sure we can find you a copy of that book really soon and I'll be you'll have read it before you go away with Geordie and Hannah in January. But you know what? If you haven't, that's ok! It can be something for you to focus on when you get back."

Jacqui nodded, smiling.

"Thanks mum!"

"So guess what happened today?" Kate asked mysteriously, cutting off some broccoli, kale and silver beet to use in the stir fry she was planning for dinner.

"What?" Jacqui asked, munching on one of the larger tomatoes that she'd picked.

"I got three phone calls about agistment," Kate replied casually, laughing at her daughter's excited look.

"Really?"

"You bet! Our prayers have been paying off!" she stated with a smile.

"So are they bringing horses? What sort? Do you think they'll be owned by people my age? How did they find out about us?"

Kate laughed at her daughter's enthusiastic questions.

"I'm not sure is the answer to the first question. Two of the calls were people just inquiring about costs, and if we had any facilities. The third was a mother who isn't happy with their current facilities as she doesn't feel the horses are looked after unless she or her kids are there. I assured her that we are home every morning and afternoon and that we would check their horses twice a day if they chose to agist with us."

"So, is she going to bring her horses? And how many does she have?"

"She has two and she said she'd get back to me. She wasn't too sure about the fact that we only had a round yard and tie up area so far. I pointed out that horses could be worked on any area where there's enough flat ground but she didn't seem too sure. We'll just have to pray that God will bring us the right clients, in the right time. He's got free reign over our lives," Kate stated, content.

"Free rein... like in the reins on a bridle?" Jacqui asked, causing her mum to smile.

"Not quite. This kind of reign is spelt with a 'g' before the 'n'. And it means that he's in control, like a king. A king reigns over his kingdom."

Jacqui nodded, smiling.

"That's a new word for me! Well I'll be praying tonight that God helps that woman to choose our property."

"You could pray right now if you wanted to," Kate encouraged, smiling when her daughter's face lit up at the idea.

"Oh yeah!"

The pair finished collecting from the veggie garden and headed inside to where the air conditioner was keeping the house cool. Jacqui asked after her brother as she helped her mum clean the vegetables to be used for dinner.

"Need you ask?" Kate questioned with a smile, "he and Kara are out at the supermarket. I think Ross said she needed to buy some new chaps for riding. The poor boy can't get away from horse crazy females."

Jacqui laughed.

"Maybe not, but I don't think he'd go shopping for horse stuff with me!"

"I don't think so either. Kara must be a special girl," Kate suggested with a small smile.

"So! Have you, Geordie and Hannah decided on what you need to take when you'll be visiting Hannah's aunt's place?"

Jacqui smiled, thrilled for the change in topic. She couldn't wait for this year to end and the next to start!

Twelve

The school term ended in late December for the girls. Jacqui had been upset to find that Ross finished school a two full weeks before her. He reminded her that that was something for her to look forward to when she started high school.

Jacqui thought that was easy for her brother to say when she was completing grade six the following year! He still had a year of finishing school earlier before she reached high school.

The now eleven year old was looking forward to being in the oldest year level in her school. She was also looking forward to completing primary school with her new horsey friends. But before then, she was looking forward to a couple of weeks in the New Year with her friends, riding ponies!

Hannah had been concerned about whether the trip would be too much for Jacqui because of her lack of riding experience. Jacqui consequently had felt it necessary to tell Hannah of the lessons she'd been keeping secret from her.

She'd thought Hannah would be upset. Instead Hannah was relieved to find that her new friend wouldn't feel left out and would be up to riding. She'd excitedly asked Jacqui about her riding. The young blonde had been proud to be able to say that she could happily walk, trot and canter by herself on their neighbour's horse. She mentioned that she'd also recently started jumping – just small jumps though.

Hannah had been ecstatic. Jacqui was glad to find that Hannah was no longer jealous of her and that her parents property hadn't ruined them being able to become good friends.

In fact, she thought that it had helped things. Jacqui really looked forward to Hannah – and possibly Geordie – being able to keep their ponies at Genesis. She realised that she looked forward to this, even if she didn't have a pony of her own to ride with them.

Now on the last day of school the three were eagerly planning their time away and what they would take. Riding boots and helmets were an absolute must, as well as sensible riding clothes in the anticipated hot weather.

Hannah informed the girls that she'd asked for a head collar and lead for Christmas and that she would be taking this along to her aunt's to see if it matched her future pony, whichever pony it was! Geordie and Jacqui gave Hannah an early birthday present in the form of a grooming kit. They'd manage to find a set of brushes that were purple, the brunette's favourite colour. Hannah smiled in delight.

"Thank you so much!"

She hugged each of her friends, telling them that owning a pony felt so real to her now that she had items that would be used on him or her. Geordie nodded in agreement, not certain but pretty sure that she too would soon have a pony.

The three girls had been working hard to keep Geordie on track. They hoped that it would pay off in the way they wanted.

Geordie had attended church a few more times with Jacqui and her family that year, finding that she easily made friends with the other kids at church. She told Jacqui that she also liked the things they talked about in kid's church.

Jacqui was pleased. She related this information to her mother, Kate smiling and encouraging her daughter to pray for her friends.

That Friday afternoon the girls finished an hour early at school because it was the end of year. They concluded that this meant that they could spend a little bit more time hanging out at Genesis. This suited all three of them just fine.

They were dropped off at the bus stop at the end of the street and then had a five minute walk down the long road that Jacqui lived on. Jacqui looked up in surprise as a horse float drove past them.

"It's going into your property!" Geordie exclaimed.

Jacqui looked to her two friends with a grin.

"Maybe we've finally got our first customers!"

Hannah was the first one to start running. Giggling, Jacqui and Geordie raced after her, keen to meet the horse that would be staying at Genesis.

The girls arrived at the front gate a couple of minutes later, out of breath. They had turned up in time to see a fat black Shetland pony being backed out of the float. Jacqui smiled in delight as she took in the sight of the older girl leading the fat pony away.

Surely that pony can't be for her to ride! She continued watching in surprise as a scuffling noise came from the float. *There's another one!*

A taller, more elegant pony was unloaded, this time by a boy. Jacqui looked over the chestnut gelding with four white socks in admiration.

"He's beautiful," she breathed out, causing the girl to smile.

"Thanks! Sox always draws attention with his colour and markings. Little Magik here gets the exclamations of, 'oh, he's so cute!' instead," she stated with a smile.

"So who rides Magik?" Geordie asked, dying to know.

"Oh, he's for our little sister Meagan. She's just learning to ride. Mum wouldn't let her until she turned five. And Sox is mine," she stated proudly, looking over to the gelding that the young boy held onto.

"So on the phone Kate said we should put them into the driveway paddock. Which one's that?"

The three girls pointed behind them. Jacqui rushed over to open the gate, holding it for the pair as they took their ponies through. They pointed them back to face the gate before they unclipped the leads.

The ponies took off in a high stepping trot, snorting loudly through their nostrils. Sox carried his tail high, showing off.

"Will you leave their head collars on?" Jacqui asked curiously.

"No. We'll take them off before we go so that they can't get them caught on anything. I just like to know that they're easy to catch if we want them while we're here. So... where are your horses?" the girl asked, looking around.

Jacqui grinned.

"Actually, we don't have any! I'm Jacqui, my mum is Kate," she offered her hand, shaking the girl's.

"Oh! I'm Alice and my brother is Andrew. Meagan's in the car..." the girl with the light brown hair said, looking to Hannah and Geordie.

The girls introduced themselves, Hannah proudly stating that she was getting a pony in the New Year. The girls chattered away for a bit, Kate coming out to talk with Alice's mum about agistment rates and details.

Jacqui had a chance to point out the round yard that her dad and brother had been building and the place where an arena was planned. Alice was enthusiastic about this idea, saying that she really liked dressage.

Shortly after the car of four people said their goodbyes and drove away.

"Your first clients are really nice!" Geordie stated happily as she watched them head back down the drive of Genesis.

Jacqui nodded, in agreement.

"So I've just realised that when we bring my pony back here – and maybe one for Geordie – that we won't be the only customers! Maybe we should make it a little project for us to find more people that can get ponies and keep them here," Hannah suggested, causing Jacqui to laugh.

"I love that idea! Do you think we could add me to that list?"

Geordie laughed.

"I sure hope so! It only makes sense that the daughter of the property owner has a pony to ride in her own backyard!"

The three girls stood at the gate to the driveway paddock for some time, watching Magik and Sox grazing contentedly. Kate put the folder of signed agistment papers down in the tie up area and then stood with them, sighing happily.

"It just looks right, doesn't it?" she asked no one in particular, "and it'll look even better when each paddock has horses."

Jacqui nodded enthusiastically.

"So were they the people that rang the other day?"

Kate smiled and nodded.

"And do you know what? They found our website online and contacted me through that... but they actually found out about our property through your friend Kara. It sounds like she's doing a good job of telling people about the agistment place next door to her!"

Jacqui laughed in delight.

"That's so cool! I wonder if she goes to school with Alice... they seemed about the same age."

Kate nodded, agreeing.

"Perhaps you can ask Kara when you have your lesson on Saturday. So! Are you girls happy that the school year is finished?" she asked with a knowing smile.

"Are you kidding? Of course we are!" Geordie responded enthusiastically.

"I think this is going to be the best school holidays yet," Hannah stated with a dreamy smile on her face, "we get to ride lots and lots at my aunt's place and then we get to bring back one or two ponies to live here at Genesis and spend the rest of our holidays playing with them! Could life be any better?"

Kate looked at the three girls, their faces filled with excitement. She smiled thinking that life was indeed as sweet for them at that moment as it possibly could be. God was good.

About the Author

Christine Meunier considers herself introduced to the wonderful world of horses at the late age of 13 when her parents agreed to lease a horse for her. She started experiencing horses via books from a young age and continues to do so, but recognises that horses cannot be learnt solely from books.

She has been studying horses from age 16, starting with the Certificate II in Horse Studies. She completed the Bachelor of Equine Science in 2015.

Christine has worked at numerous thoroughbred studs in Australia as well as overseas in Ireland for a breeding season.

She then gained experience in a couple of Melbourne based horse riding schools, instructing at a basic level before heading off overseas again, this time to South Africa to spend hours in the saddle of endurance and trail horses on the Wild Coast.

Particularly passionate about the world of breeding horses, she writes a blog about equine education which you can view at http://equus-blog.com/

You can contact Christine via email at christine@christinemeunierauthor.com.

Sign up to her author news and receive updates – and freebies – as they are available! http://eepurl.com/bAiMpL

Every effort is made to ensure that this book is free of spelling and grammatical errors. That said, I am only

103

human! If you find any errors, I'd love to know so that I can correct them. You can contact me at christine@christinemeunierauthor.com with details of any issues you may find.

Printed in Great Britain
by Amazon

77548242R00068